SILENCE IS  DEADLY

A Novel By
SHARON STEFAN

Copyright © 2023 by Sharon A. Stefan

First Edition 2023
All rights reserved.

No part of this publication may be reproduced in any form, or by any means, electronic or mechanical, including photocopying, recording, or any information browsing, storage or retrieval system, without permission in writing from the author.

This is a work of fiction. Names, characters, places, and incidents are products of the author's imagination or are used fictitiously and are not to be construed as real. Any resemblance to actual events, locales, organizations, or person, living or dead, is entirely coincidental.

Print ISBN: 979-8-35091-768-0
eBook ISBN: 979-8-35091-769-7

For Mumsie

PROLOGUE

Trevor

(Friday, June 8)

EIGHT-YEAR-OLD TREVOR RACED ALONG the sidewalk of the foggy lakeside village riding the old, blue CCM bike he found tossed by the roadside two years ago. They were as inseparable now as a boy with his faithful dog. His heart pounded. He lifted one white-knuckled hand off the handlebar and swiped at the tears trickling down his cheeks.

Pa had come home from work drunk, as usual. However, this time he was like a wounded rhino stumbling into the house, his beady, bloodshot eyes glaring at Trevor. "What are you looking at?" he spat, making his way into the kitchen.

"God damn Seymour Harding, ruining my life again."

Ma approached him, laying her hand on his arm. "What's wrong?"

"That asshole is shutting down the plant and moving the whole fucking operation to another city, miles away. That's what's wrong," he said, raising his voice. "I'll be out of work and so will half the village."

"Oh no, Joe!" she said, looking at him, body tense, brows furrowed. "I'm so sorry." Her eyes lingered on him, unsure of what to say next that wouldn't set him off. Hesitantly, she nudged him toward the table. "Come, sit down and have a cup of coffee while I heat up your dinner."

He turned on her, eyes narrowing to angry slits, and shoved her away. "Coffee, my ass!"

She stumbled, hit the kitchen table, and landed dazed and confused on the faded linoleum floor. Trevor's six-year-old twin brothers, having milk and cookies before bed, sprang up from the milk-spattered table and bolted from the room. His baby sister, hands covering her ears, stood in the middle of the room crying. Her eyes were closed, and a facecloth— her security blanket—dangled from the corner of her mouth.

Trevor rushed outside, grabbed his bicycle leaning against the side of the house, and took off. He *had* to reach his older brother, who worked at the mushroom farm Friday nights after school. Dylan would know what to do!

Trevor lifted his butt off the seat and leaned forward over the handlebars, back flat, elbows dropped—his feet peddling a mile a minute up the hill. His curly ginger hair bounced around as if it were alive. At the top, he plopped back down in the seat and continued sailing on down the other side under the eerie glow of the street lamps. Right through the hazy red glow of the town's one traffic light. It was the beginning of June, and the hordes of summer tourists hadn't infested the village yet.

The fog made all that had been bright and cheerful during the day, now grey and gloomy. With no breeze, the still, heavy air kept the formidable stink from the mushroom farm pressed down, covering everything like a putrid blanket. He was just about in line with the United Church, when he decided to cut across the road. He gave the handlebars a quick jerk upward, jumped his bike over the curb and onto the road heading for McCleary Street and the farm two miles up.

Straining to see through his tears, he dug his fist into his eyes. When he looked back up, all he could see were two giant, blinding orbs of light coming straight at him.

CHAPTER ONE

Brynn

(Friday, June 8)

I'D HIT THE WALL— borrowing my late Grandma Mumsie's favorite expression, often heard when, as a preteen, my friends and I would drag her around the mall, the zoo, the amusement park—anywhere kids liked to go. Now, at only thirty-four, I could empathize with that feeling. I was more than ready to call it quits, go home, and crash into bed.

The quiet in the church dining hall after the fundraising dinner was almost palpable, compared to a short while ago, when it was noisier than Saturday lunchtime at the mall food court. The only sound now was the occasional clatter of dishes or burst of laughter coming from the adjacent kitchen. I took one last look around the room to make sure all the dishes had been collected from the long, vinyl-covered wooden tables. Spotting a dish way down at the back, I wandered down, rolling my neck from side to side, trying to get the kinks out. A plate lay there, with a knife and fork crossed in the middle. It brought a smile to my face thinking of my Irish Gran again. If Mumsie were here today, she'd shake her head, *tsking*, cross herself, then quickly separate the offending cutlery. She insisted people place their cutlery side-by-side when finished eating, not crossed, which is bad luck. Good old Gran knew and believed in just about every silly superstition there was. I grabbed the ill-omened utensils and plate and headed for the kitchen.

With one hand covering my mouth, trying to hide a gigantic yawn, I elbowed my way through the swing door. It surprised me to see the hands on the clock over the kitchen sink inching towards 9:00 p.m.

Four of my five companions—Sophie, Georgie, Edda, and Trish were hard at work. The fifth, Kaydee Wiebe, was slouched down at the gray Formica-topped table in the corner gasping and wheezing. You wouldn't know she was the youngest of our group at twenty-six. Heavyset and asthmatic, Kaydee tended to limit her physical activity. You wouldn't find her running laps along the track by the high school where she taught grades eleven and twelve English and math. However, to her credit, she was always willing to pitch in and help out whenever she could.

She grabbed her oversized canvas tote bag, rummaged around inside, and pulled out her inhaler. After giving it a couple of good shakes, she removed the cap, put it up to her mouth, and depressed the pump. Almost instantly, her wheezing began to ease up.

I walked over and touched her shoulder. "Kaydee, are you okay?"

Elbow on the table, cradling her head in her hand, she just nodded not bothering to look up.

Concerned, I leaned in closer. "Why don't you go home now... we're almost finished here."

She took in a deep breath and continued to sit. Not knowing what else to say, I gave her shoulder a comforting squeeze, then looked back up to see what the other women were doing.

Sophie was busy scraping food scraps off the pile of dirty dishes. She then handed the dishes over to Georgie, who loaded them into one of the two industrial-strength dishwashers.

Over by the maintenance closet, Trish was busy tying up several large, green-plastic garbage bags, getting them ready to take out back to the trash bins. And last but not least, Edda was at the sink scrubbing pots and pans, too big to fit into either dishwasher, up to her elbows in soapy water.

I saw her glance out the window above the sink. Suddenly, in mid-scrub, she froze—her jaw dropped, and her eyes bulged. She let go of the large pot she was holding, splashing sudsy water all over herself, the counter, and the floor. Then, as if trying to stop whatever she was witnessing, her hands shot up in the air. Seconds later, we all heard the squealing of brakes and a loud . . . *thump*.

"Oh, my God," she cried, her soapy hands clutching her face.

I rushed over, moved her aside, and looked out the window. Not seeing anything, I turned back to her. "What is it? What's happened?" When there was no response, just a deer in the headlights look, I gently shook her by the shoulders.

Edda finally looked at me, her face as white as her apron. "Oh, God! A car..." she stammered, trying to get the words out. "A car just hit a child on a bike."

The other women stopped what they were doing and hurried over.

"Call 911!" I shouted to Trish as I dashed outside.

The others followed close on my heels, except for Kaydee, who plodded along well behind the rest of us, trying to catch her breath. A twisted, mangled bike lay next to the curb under a streetlight. A short distance away in a heap in the shadows, a child lay like a broken toy. His limbs were bent unnaturally, and his head was turned so that the innocent face, eyes open and vacant, stared up at us over a bony shoulder blade. You could tell at once the child was dead.

Sophie's hand flew up to her mouth. "Good Lord! I think I recognize this laddie. He's one of the Chadwick bairns, Trevor, I believe."

Trish came running out of the church, her short, vivid-red hair visible under the streetlamp, even through the dense fog. "The ambulance and police are on their way," she shouted, hurrying over to where we were standing. When she saw the body in the grass, she quickly turned and started praying. For a long moment, we all just stood there, eyes downcast, speechless. Even though it was a warm night, I shivered, a chill running down my spine.

"Edda, were you able to get a look at the car?" I asked, surprised by the trembly, high-pitched words coming out of my mouth. In the distance, we could hear the wail-of-sirens coming from over the treetops. Edda stared at me as if trying to grasp my question.

"Uh, not a really good look. I . . ." The sirens, much louder now, cut her off.

The ambulance materialized out of the misty veil and swerved around the corner, blue lights flashing. The sound trailed off to a *wee-waaah* as the vehicle approached and stopped in front of us, the police cruiser right behind. Two paramedics jumped out of the ambulance and rushed over to where the boy lay. After checking for signs of life and not finding any, they looked back, shaking their heads, and waved the police chief over, who had just emerged from his cruiser. He hurried over to join them.

We were all huddled together for support when Police Chief Charlie Boyd finally approached us. He tipped his hat, his face grave.

"Did any of you ladies see what happened?"

"I did," said Edda, her chin trembling. "I was looking out the window …" she hid her face in her hands and started sobbing. After regaining her composure, she continued. "The boy was crossing the road on his bike, when a car came racing out of the fog and hit him! It stopped for a minute, then just sped away."

"Did you get a good look at the car?" Chief Boyd asked.

"Couldn't see much through the fog, but I could tell that it was a big car, and black, I think."

"What make was it?"

Edda shrugged. "I don't know cars."

"What about the driver? Did you get a look at them? Young, old? Anything?"

"No. It all happened so fast," Edda responded trying to justify herself."

"Did anyone else see anything?" Chief Boyd scanned our faces. He knew us from church. He and his wife had regularly attended Sunday service, but, since her death two years ago, he'd become a stranger.

"Edda was the only one looking out the window at the time," I said.

"I'm sure the wee laddie's name is Trevor Chadwick," Sophie volunteered.

Chief Boyd scribbled in his notebook, then eyed Edda. "I'll need a written statement from you Edda." Noticing her tired, tear-stained face, he said, "we don't have to do it now. I'll come by your house in the morning and get it then. In the meantime, try and think if there is something else you can remember, anything at all to distinguish the vehicle. I realize how upsetting this is." He looked around at the rest of us. "I guess unless there's anything else you ladies can tell me, you might as well go home." He waited. When all he got was a few muffled sobs and silence, he turned and hurried back to the police cruiser, grabbing the radio.

I looked at Edda. "I don't think you're in any shape to drive right now. I'll drive you home and we can pick your car up tomorrow."

"Thanks, I'd appreciate that." She sniffled, dapping her eyes with the tissue Kaydee handed her.

We headed back inside the church to pick up our belongings. Sophie offered to lock up, and come back in the morning to finish cleaning up. At one-inch shy of five feet, she might have been small, but at eighty years of age, she still had more energy than most folks half her age and twice her size—earning her the nickname Mighty Mouse.

I knew Sam would be wondering why I wasn't home yet, so pardoning myself, I pulled my phone out of my purse and called him. He was sleeping when I left the house this morning. And knowing I had a busy day ahead of me, I had quickly showered, put my face on, and twisted my long chestnut hair back into a knotted ponytail. After giving him a peck on the cheek, I slipped quietly from the room. Lucky for me, the fur ball curled up at the foot end of our bed just lifted his head, flopped it back down, and went back to sleep.

This tragic news shocked Sam. I told him not to bother waiting up for me, as I was driving Edda home, and wouldn't be getting back until late.

Slipping my phone back into my purse, I turned back to the group. After hugs and sobs all around, we said our final goodbyes and dispersed into the sadness of the night.

Edda leaned forward in the passenger seat, eyes closed and shaking her head. "It was all going so well tonight; the dinner turnout was better than expected, and then this horrible, horrible thing. That poor child. I can't imagine what his parents will be going through tonight." She put her seat belt on, glancing over at me. "Do you think we should go over there and try to comfort them?"

"I think we should leave it to Chief Boyd," I said, pulling onto the road. "He'll contact Reverend Kudhill, and they'll look after notifying the Chadwicks." After a pause, I asked, "You can't remember anything else about the car?"

She drew in a heavy sigh. "It was a large black car... but something about it did seem vaguely familiar."

As I pulled the car up to a stop sign, lights from an approaching vehicle flooded the front seat. I stole a look at her just as her head snapped up, a puzzled expression on her face.

"You know," she said, "I think there was writing on the side of the car."

My eyes locked on hers for a split second before returning to the road.

Silence. Then . . . "Oh, my God, Brynn! I think I know whose car that was!"

Grabbing the wheel tighter, I turned and stared at her. "Who?"

Her hazel eyes grew impossibly wide as she stared back at me in realization. "That was Seymour Harding's car! His company car, with the *Harding Meat Packers* logo on the door— I can't believe he didn't stop."

My eyes returned to the road, my jaw hanging open. "Are you sure? Seymour Harding? *The* Seymour Harding—church trustee, big shot in town? No way!"

We drove the last few kilometres in silence, trying to make sense out of what made no sense. I made a turn and pulled the car off the main road and headed down the long, winding, gravel driveway leading to the Hendrik's dairy farm. The front porch light was on—a beacon of light in the misty darkness. As we climbed the steps to the front door, I noticed a breeze had come up, making an eerie sound as the tree branches scratched together.

Edda fished around in her purse for her keys; it slipped from her hands. She bent over, picked it up, and continued digging around inside. Finally, she pulled the keys out and stuck one in the door.

"Henk's not home," she said. "He and the boys are at the 4H conference in Ottawa. They left after this evening's milking and won't be back now until Wednesday."

"I can spend the night here if you like?" I offered, a strained smile on my face.

Edda sighed. "Thanks, but... I'm being silly. I'll be okay." She opened the door, and I followed her in.

We both needed to calm down and unwind. I watched her as she drifted into the living room and sunk into the couch, then I went into the kitchen to make us some tea.

I squeezed my eyes shut, then opened them wide in an effort to stay awake. While I puttered around in the kitchen, the day replayed in my head. This morning, I made my regular pit-stop at the Timmy's drive-through and bought a medium cafe latte, then drove to my health food shop fifty kilometres down the road. After opening the store and getting it ready for the day ahead, I took an inventory of the supplies on hand. Around noon, I left my assistant Lori-Anne in charge and hurried back to the Hubbs Harbour United Church, where I've been helping out with this evening's fundraising dinner—cooking, serving, and cleaning up. I bit down on my lower lip, thinking what a dreadful way to end the day!

When the tea was ready, I put the cups, teapot, spoons, milk, and sugar on a tray, and carried it out to the living room.

Edda, slouched down into the couch, quickly sat up as I brought the tray in.

"I just can't believe Seymour Harding didn't stop," I said, putting the tray down on the coffee table and pouring the tea. "It's not like him. He's a trustee of the church, for heaven's sake. He must have been so shocked he wasn't thinking straight." I added milk to my cup and stirred. "He's hopefully realized what he's done and has gone to the police by now."

Edda sipped at her tea, hands wrapped around the cup for warmth and to keep them from shaking. She stared at me. "Maybe he doesn't even realize he hit that child—in the fog and all." She set her cup down on the coffee table and stood up. "I guess I better call Chief Boyd and tell him about the logo." She eyed me for encouragement.

I looked over my shoulder at the antique Napoleon-hat-style clock on the fireplace mantle; it was just past midnight. "It's late, why don't you wait and tell him when he comes by later this morning to get your witness statement? It's best you try to get some sleep now."

But I had a funny feeling neither of us would be getting much sleep tonight.

CHAPTER TWO

Edda

(Saturday, June 9)

EDDA HEARD TIRES CRUNCHING on the gravel driveway out front and knew Police Chief Boyd had arrived. She was awake most of the night, unable to get the vision of the poor, dead child out of her head. Now, just the thought of having to dredge up last night's accident brought a queasy feeling to the pit of her stomach.

She pushed aside the lacy Dutch curtain covering the front door window, a souvenir her mother brought back from Holland five years ago, and peeked out. Then watched as Police Chief Boyd got out of his cruiser and made his way up the porch steps.

She opened the door even before he knocked.

He nodded and tipped his hat, a half-formed smile on his face; "Mornin, Edda," he said.

She stepped aside and invited him in. As he entered the house, he took off his hat, revealing a buzz-cut of fair hair with a receding "M" hairline. Then, tucking his hat under his arm, he wiped his boots off on the doormat. He glanced around the kitchen. "Coffee sure smells good."

"Just made. Would you like a cup?" she offered, motioning for him to take a seat at the table.

"Thanks, I'd love one," he said.

She watched as he walked over and put his hat down on the old, pock-marked but well-loved pine table and his briefcase down on the floor. He then leaned over, opened the case, and withdrew the paperwork.

Charlie, in his mid-fifties, was built like a barn, with just the beginnings of a potbelly hanging over his shiny black belt. She'd remembered how hard he had taken his wife's death two years ago from cancer. His wife had once confided in her that with their son living out in Edmonton and Charlie's mind always miles away on one case or another, even when he was home, the house felt empty.

Edda felt blessed having her husband and their two boys—young men now, in their twenties—all working on their family dairy farm. She couldn't imagine an empty house. It was hard to have her 'men' away for even a few days.

After his wife's diagnosis, Charlie spent much more time at home, until the day came when she needed to go into hospice care. Then he became as much of a fixture in her room at the hospice facility as the bedside table lamp. Upon her death, he worked even harder. Now, his job really was his life. Edda felt sorry for him, and secretly kept an eye open for all eligible single or widowed women she thought would make a good match.

She brought the coffee mugs over to the table and sat down. From all the church events he'd attended, she didn't need to ask him how he took his coffee—black, two sugars. Steam rose from his cup.

SILENCE IS ~~GOLDEN~~ DEADLY

Blowing on it, he took a tentative sip. "I didn't see any sign of Henk or the boys outside."

"No. They're away at a conference for a few days, so I'm on my own."

"This won't take long. I'm sure you have lots to do around the farm."

"I couldn't sleep," she said, looking into his steely blue eyes. "I was up before the cock crowed. Had the chickens and goats fed and the milking started even before our farmhand arrived. I guess not sleeping has its benefits." She took a sip of her coffee. "Brynn will be coming by later this afternoon to give me a lift into town to get my car. She gave me a ride home last night. I was so distraught. We all were."

He raised his cup. "Perfect coffee, Edda. I can give you a lift back to town when we're finished here if you like?"

"Thanks for the offer, Charlie, but I think I'll wait for Brynn." Her eyes crinkled at the corners. "How would it look, me getting out of a police cruiser!"

Charlie, trying not to laugh, almost choked on his coffee. He quickly wiped his mouth with his hanky and then pulled a pen from his shirt pocket. Putting the pen on top of the papers, he slid them toward her. "Edda, this is the witness statement, fill it out as best you can. It's important you write down all you remember seeing and hearing last night."

Edda began filling out the forms. After a couple of pages, she looked up and noticed Charlie gazing around the kitchen. This was her favourite room of the house—it's heart and soul. She loved the way the sunlight danced off the thick golden-hued maple countertops, bringing a warm glow into the room. Baskets of garden-fresh herbs and brown eggs gathered this morning sat beside the large, white enamel-coated cast iron farm sink. On the walls hung Dutch-themed blue-and-white plates depicting pictures of windmills, with farmers wearing wooden clogs out working in their fields.

Getting back to filling out the forms, she struggled to hold back the tears. She wanted to forget the boy lying on the grass with the blank stare on his little face, knowing he would never be going home to *his* family.

Finally finished, she sat back, eyes closed. When she opened them, she noticed Charlie's cup was empty and offered him a refill.

"No thanks Edda," he said, as he pushed himself away from the table. "I best be going." He looked over the completed forms, making sure they were signed, then stuffed them into his briefcase.

She cleared her throat. "What if I forgot something, that I remember later?"

"No problem—you can always contact me." He reached into his briefcase and pulled out a leaflet titled "Giving a Witness Statement—What Happens Next?" and handed it to her. "Everything you need to know is in this leaflet: who to contact, telephone numbers, and, if you have to, going to court."

He made his way to the front door, thanking her for the coffee. "Edda, so far, you're our only witness. We're still canvassing the area, but so far, we've come up with nothing. With what little you could tell us, unless there's any new information, you might not hear from us for a while."

She watched as he got into his cruiser and drove away. She felt guilty about not mentioning the logo—why, why hadn't she told him about the logo—*she had planned to!*

Still, she had this gut feeling that Seymour would do the right thing and come forward. With her head starting to throb, she went over to the sink, grabbed the aspirin bottle, and tossed back a couple of pills—then shrugged; what harm would it do to give Seymour another day or two?

CHAPTER THREE

Brynn

(Saturday, June 9)

THAT AFTERNOON, I LEFT my health food shop in the capable hands of my shop assistant, Lori-Anne, but first, I went up and down the aisles, picking up items for the dinner I was making at the Chadwicks' tonight. I hoped our store's famous gluten-free, extra-cheesy mac and cheese might take the kids' minds off the loss of their brother—if only long enough for them to eat something.

On my way back to Hubbs Harbour, I stopped by the Hendricks farm and picked up Edda. She slid into the passenger seat beside me, put her seat belt on, and glanced over at me.

"Afternoon, Brynn," she said, not smiling. Then she sat there—straight back, knees pressed together, gripping her purse in her lap, staring straight ahead.

"*So*—how did it go this morning?" I asked.

"Okay," she shrugged.

I pulled out of the driveway and headed towards town. "I guess it was pretty tough giving that eye-witness report."

"Yes, yes it was."

I noticed Edda wasn't her usual chatty self, lips tight. "I'm guessing Seymour didn't turn himself in?"

"I could have sworn he would—but no, he didn't," she answered.

"What did Chief Boyd say when you told him about the logo?"

Silence. Then . . .

"I didn't tell him."

My eyebrows shot up as I flashed a questioning glance at her.

"I was going to, but I just can't help thinking he'll turn himself in."

"Edda, the sooner you tell the police the better." I could see her fingers nervously twisting the straps on her purse. "I think you've given him enough time."

"Yes, I guess you're right," she muttered.

It wasn't far from the Hendriks' farm into town. The rest of our drive was quiet. We passed by the winding dirt road leading north to the alpaca farm. A smile crossed my face seeing the mop-topped, buck-toothed, comically cute alpacas grazing on the hilltop. I felt almost guilty, given the current tragic circumstances. But it was hard not to appreciate all the beauty the county had to offer. Moving here from the city five years ago, after my two miscarriages in as many years, was the best decision Sam and I could have made. I was feeling depressed and couldn't focus on my job. I—we—needed a change. With the county's scenery, fresh produce, sandy beaches, farms, and wineries, to name a few of its many offerings—this was our chance at a new beginning.

Just as we pulled into the church parking lot, I remembered, "Oh, Reverend Jim called earlier. He wants me to arrange visits from our women's C.I.A [Christians in Action] group to help out at the Chadwicks. I'm on my way over there now. I'll be making dinner for them, and Sophie will be coming by later in the evening to bathe and put the kids to bed. Let me know what day is good for you."

With a nod, Edda hauled herself from the car. "Thanks for the ride. I'll call you," she yelled back heading for her car.

I poked my head out the window. "See you at church tomorrow."

The Chadwicks' small two-story house had seen better days: white paint flaking off the clapboards exposed multi-coloured paint layers beneath, torn screens covered the dirty windows, and toys in various stages of neglect and disrepair littered the long, weedy front lawn.

I headed up the steps lugging my bags of groceries. Putting one down, I opened the loose, rickety screened door. I could just imagining the punishment it got from the kids continually flinging it open. After knocking a few times and getting no answer, I decided to try around back.

Setting the bags down on the back stoop, I looked through the smudgy window and saw Betty hunched in a chair at the kitchen table staring into space, her brassy blonde hair framing a tired-looking face. She looked rail-thin and drained, much older than her thirty-eight years, as if the lifeblood had been sucked out of her. Between her finger-tips, a cigarette trailed a train of ashes over the edge of a heavy-looking glass ashtray.

A little carrot-topped ragamuffin stood beside her, tugging on her housecoat, desperate to get her attention. I could hear a baby's crying coming from somewhere inside the house. Betty ignored them both.

I tapped on the glass a few times. "Betty! Betty, it's Brynn, Brynn Grant," I called out, finally breaking her spell.

She glanced up and nodded. Then, stubbing out her cigarette, she slowly stood up, hefted the little girl to her hip, and made her way to the door.

As the door opened, I suppressed a gasp; just under Betty's eye was an ugly bruise, and not having seen her daughter before, I was shocked to see a large, raised, purplish-blue birthmark covering one side of the child's face. My heart ached.

Managing a weak smile, I greeted her, then carried the bags into the kitchen and plopped them down on the counter. I turned back to Betty. "Are you okay?"

Head down, avoiding my look of concern, she said, "I don't know—I just feel so tired." She ambled over to the counter with the little girl clinging barnacle-like to her side. "Would you like something to drink? Coffee? I only have instant." There was a hint of apology in her voice.

"Instant sounds just great. Here, let me get it," I said, guiding Betty back to the table. After I settled her back in her chair with the little girl now nestled on her lap, I went back and plugged in the kettle, unpacked the groceries, and made the coffee.

When I finally brought the cups over to the table, Betty appeared miles away. The little girl on her mother's lap, content now, chewing away on her face cloth.

"Where are the other kids?" I asked.

It took a moment for her to respond. "The twins, Erick and Ernie are down the road playing street hockey with their friends, the baby is upstairs, and God only knows where Dylan is. Teenagers, who can keep track of them?"

I took a sip of coffee, "How old are the twins?"

"Six," she answered, staring into her cup.

I smiled down at the little girl, now gazing up at me with big green moppet eyes. A wave of pity hit me again as I looked at that little disfigured angelic face.

"And what's your name sweetie?" I asked.

A hint of a smile crossed her face just before she turned her head, burying it in her mother's sweater.

"I know what you'd like," I said, getting up and going over to the counter. I pulled out a bag of our store's delicious chocolate chip cookies, brought one over and handed it to her. "Here you go. Can you tell me your name now?"

She hesitantly took the cookie, mumbling something inaudible.

Betty answered robotically for her. "Deedee."

All was quiet again, except for the ticking of the wall clock. I had forgotten all about the baby I had heard crying earlier—until the crying started up again. Tilting my head, I looked over at Betty, who seemed content to just ignore it.

I cleared my throat. "Would you like me to go check on the baby?"

She nodded. "He's upstairs."

SILENCE IS ~~GOLDEN~~ DEADLY

I hurried up the stairs and followed the crying into one of the bedrooms. It contained a queen-sized bed, which I assumed was Betty and Joe's, and over in one corner was a twin bed—probably Deedee's, since it had a girlish, Disney-themed *Frozen* comforter on it—and in a far corner was the baby's crib.

The baby was lying on his back, his face purple... wizened like an old man from all the crying. The pungent odor almost knocked me over.

"Whew, poor baby!" I winced, wrinkling my nose. "Boy, do you need a diaper change."

In my arms, the baby's howling softened to a mere whimper. He was a mess. I couldn't help wondering how long he'd been left like this. After I found baby wipes and a fresh diaper, I changed him and picking him up, headed for the stairs. Passing a partially opened door, I poked my head into the room. It had bunk beds, each covered with identical rocket-ship comforters, and on the opposite wall was another twin bed, draped in a Spider-Man blanket. Given the cartoonish bedspreads and toys tossed about the room, I assumed the young twin boys and Trevor slept here.

I continued to snoop, finding myself in front of the bathroom. It was small, hardly adequate for six kids and two adults. The shower curtain was torn and dangled from the bar above the tub. Another room was by the stairs—the size of a closet, with a double bed jammed in wall-to-wall. Grotesque pictures of punk bands—with musicians sporting gel-spiked hair, their tongues hanging out and body piercings everywhere—were taped to the walls. A teenager's room.

On my way back into the kitchen, I spotted a bassinette on the floor and put the baby inside. Once in the kitchen, I set to work finding his bottle and heating up the milk. Meanwhile, Betty seemed not to notice I'd taken over her kitchen and was fussing over her baby—now contentedly nursing away on his bottle, a hand towel propped underneath holding it up. I finally sat down at the table and took a sip of my now-cold coffee. "What's the baby's name?" I asked Betty.

Little Deedee gazed up at me with a big grin, a gap showing between her front teeth, cookie crumbs stuck around her mouth, and said what sounded like "Airy".

"Arti," Betty said. "It's really Arthur, but we call him Arti." There was a moment's silence, as Betty shook her head, looking down at the floor. "Trevor was such a good boy. He always helped me around the house. Whenever I needed anything from the store, he never argued, he just jumped on his bike and went and got it." Tears welled up in her eyes.

"Joe came home drunk last night. He got more and more angry and belligerent. I've never seen him like that." She gingerly touched the bruise under her eye. "He'll be losing his job when the meat plant closes its doors at the end of the month. All the employees will. After fifty years in the county, it's shutting down. Joe says it's because of the union he helped organize—I remember how honoured he was when they chose him to be shop steward. Seymour was dead set against the employees organizing a union. I guess the last straw was the strike the union had last year asking for better wage and safer working conditions."

"Betty, I'm so sorry." I put my hand over hers.

"I miss my Trevor so much. What am I going to do without him? My poor, poor Trevor."

She wrapped her arms around Deedee, rocking back and forth, tears streaking down her cheeks. "My poor children; what's to become of them?"

SILENCE IS ~~GOLDEN~~ DEADLY

"Where's Joe now?"

"Don't know. Suppose he's off on another drinking binge. Drowning his sorrows, like always." She sniffled. "Haven't seen him since he barged out of the house last night. He might not even know Trevor's dead."

"Bad news travels fast," I said. "I'm sure he's heard. I'll see if I can find out where he is. Meanwhile, the church is setting up a fund to help your family. Try not to worry about the kids; they'll be okay. It's you I'm worried about right now."

Around 8:00 that evening, there was a knock at the front door. Sophie arrived for the evening shift.

"How goes it?" she asked, stepping into the hall.

"All's well as can be, Soph. I just finished washing the dinner dishes. The kids all ate their mac and cheese. Betty never touched her food, and the older boy, Dylan, hasn't come home yet. Betty's in the kitchen. She just sits at the table, numb to all that's going on around her."

Sophie glanced into the living room where the kids were sitting on the floor in front of the TV. "Kids seem fine."

"Poor little Deedee," I said. "What a pity about her disfigurement. I've never seen a birthmark that size before."

"It's called a hemangioma, kind of a port-wine stain," Sophie said, having been a nurse for over fifty years. "Unfortunately, it's expensive to have corrective surgery done, especially on one that size, and she's now at the age when it's best to begin treatments. Much later, children have more of a sense of self, and psychological issues kick in. Also, it's best to start treatments as early as possible; it helps minimize the number and severity of surgeries required later on. The kicker is, it's not covered by insurance. It's considered cosmetic surgery."

Frowning, I shook my head. "Such a shame." I glanced back at the children settled in front of the TV. "I'm sure you'll have a quiet evening—good luck. I best get going."

I went back into the kitchen, grabbed my jacket and purse, and after checking on baby Arti, who was sleeping—well, like a baby, I said my goodbyes to Betty. "I'm leaving now. Sophie's in the living room with the kids. She'll help put them to bed.

Betty, sitting there in a world of her own, didn't answer.

I went out through the living room and said my goodbyes to Sophie and the kids, and as I opened the front door, I was surprised to see Dylan on the other side. He shuffled in, head down, hands stuffed into the pockets of his baggy jeans that were hanging off his skinny hips. He glanced our way without saying a word.

At eighteen he was tall, over six feet, and his thin, rake-like frame was topped by hair that could only be described as… conflicted. One side of his head was shaved, while the other had long, straight, jet-black hair. His facial hardware was difficult to ignore—a silver ring in each eyebrow, one through his nose, and another through his upper lip.

"Hi Dylan," I said as Sophie came up behind me in the hall.

Still looking at his feet, he mumbled something as he passed by us, then hot-footed it straight up the stairs.

CHAPTER FOUR

Dylan

(Saturday, June 9)

DYLAN THREW HIMSELF DOWN on the bed, sniffling. The corners of his mouth turned down as his lips quivered, tears pooling in his eyes—*must not cry, must not cry*, he told himself. He sat up, arms crossed, shoulders pulled together, and wiped his nose with the sleeve of his fleece hoodie. Unable to hold the tears back any longer, the floodgates opened. He grabbed his pillow, burying his face in it, and let loose.

When the tears finally subsided, leaving behind just the occasional body shudder, he took the pillow away from his face, and sat there staring at it—hypnotized.

Slowly a bittersweet, manic-looking smile crossed his face, remembering how he and Trevor used to have pillow fights and taunt each other.

"You little troll," he'd say to Trevor. "Why don't you go out and play in the traffic?"

Trevor's comeback . . . "Yah. Why don't you go play in the cemetery with your zombie friends?"

Trevor would then do his impression of the walking dead: slouched to one side, he'd shamble along, arms dangling, dragging his feet, his mouth wide open, moaning, tongue lolling about.

In fits of laughter, they'd start throwing whatever they could get their hands on: pillows, shoes, clothing, books, even food. If they were outside, it would be sticks, grass, hats, and even doggie doo. Dylan knew their laughter could be heard all the way down the street.

He wiped his face with his sleeve again—he was really going to miss his little buddy.

There was no one he could speak to about Trevor's death. His brothers and sister were too young, and his parents had major problems of their own. He was racked with guilt.

He had been up in his room with Prissy Harding Friday night—the door closed as usual. They had been listening to their favorite goth band, Slipknot, with headphones on full blast—if a space shuttle had launched from his backyard, they wouldn't have heard it!

Nobody had known they were up there. He was supposed to have been working at the mushroom farm, but he called in sick, desperate to fool around with Prissy—and not just in the back seat of a car or in the bushes at the park. They'd wanted to make out in a real bed. But, it was like *Mission Impossible*, everything had to align just right.

Pa worked late Friday nights, and since it was payday, he'd be at the Legion, guzzling beer with his mates until the wee hours of the morning, spending money they couldn't afford. He wouldn't be home until long after Prissy had gone. Good thing, as Pa hated the Harding's, especially Prissy's father, Seymour, his boss. If Pa ever found Seymour's daughter in our house, he'd hit the roof. Ma, always busy getting the kids fed or ready for bed, wouldn't even notice Prissy was in the house. And, after school on Friday nights, Trevor would be out playing with the other kids on the street.

It would work out for Pris, too. She told him her dad would be away golfing with his buds this weekend, and Lara—she hardly ever called her "Mom," always Lara—would be out playing bridge. So, they decided this was D-Day ("do it").

Arriving around 6:00, Pris texted him she was outside. He went out to meet her and not seeing her anywhere, walked down their driveway and around back of the house. He was shocked to see her getting out of her father's black Lincoln, a smile on her face as big as the car. She ran over to him and gave his arm a love punch. She was wearing a hoodie and sunglasses, and barely recognizable—looked like just another of his homie friends.

"My friend Tara bailed on giving me a ride over," she said, her frown twisting into a smile as she cocked her head to one side, grinning at him. "So, I borrowed Dad's car. He's out of town, and Lara's gone to a meeting. The keys were hanging on the key hook in the kitchen—he's never gonna know."

They had fooled around, listened to music, and were oblivious to what was going on downstairs. When it was time for Pris to leave, Dylan opened the bedroom door and stuck his head out. The coast was clear. The only sound was the television droning on in the living room. They crept downstairs, and he watched as Prissy tiptoed behind the twins, sitting cross-legged on the carpet, riveted to the flat screen. She threw Dylan a kiss and slipped out the front door.

On his way back upstairs, he heard sobs coming from the kitchen and went to check. His mom was sitting at the table with a wadded-up tissue in her hand, little Deedee stuck to her side like a burr on a dog's butt. Baby Arti in his bassinet was starting to whimper.

Dabbing at her eyes, Ma told him Pa had come home early—hammered, in a nasty temper and aching for a fight. He left about an hour ago.

∼

A short while later, there was a loud knock on the front door. Dylan opened the door to find Police Chief Boyd and Reverend Jim standing there. They stepped inside and asked to speak to his parents. Dylan ushered them in and called his mom.

Chief Boyd took off his hat and, taking a slow steady breath, looked at her. "I'm so sorry Betty, he said, his face etched with sadness, but I have bad news. Your son Trevor was in a hit-and-run accident. I'm sorry to say he didn't make it. Betty—Trevor is dead."

CHAPTER FIVE

Brynn

(Sunday, June 10)

ON OUR WAY TO church Sunday morning, Sam and I drove along the lakeshore. The sun danced off the turquoise water, dazzling like millions of diamonds beneath the cloudless, powder-blue sky. As we arrived at the church, the sweet smell from the lilac hedge filled the air. The mushroom farm odor from two days ago was long forgotten.

We climbed the wide, concrete front steps of the church. For those less agile, there was a backdoor entrance off the parking lot with an elevator just inside the door.

As we walked down the aisle greeting friends, sunlight streamed in through the three magnificent stained-glass windows. During the evening services, golden light from the setting sun cascaded in through the three sister windows on the opposite side. I had always admired the beauty and artistry of stained-glass windows in places of worship. They not only added to the architectural beauty, but starting as early as the seventh century, they were a means of telling biblical stories and depicting people from the Bible to the widespread illiterate of the time. Even the vibrant colours had meaning. Green was the colour of grass and nature, representing growth and rebirth, life over death. Violet symbolized love, truth, passion, and suffering. And white was for chastity innocence, and purity, often associated with God.

People filing in and chatting away drew my attention away from the windows. With county farms being miles apart, coming to church on Sundays was as much of a social event as hearing the preacher's sermon.

I noticed Reverend James Kudhill, a.k.a. Reverend Jim, down in the chancel, talking to a few of his parishioners. If the church was the heart of the town, then Reverend Jim was the main artery. Wearing John Lennon-style glasses, he was an engaging man in his mid-sixties, medium height and slight of build. Unbeknownst to most people, he had Tourette syndrome, although anyone could see he had facial tics. Sophie, who knew everything about everybody in the county, had filled me in about his condition. Before retiring from her nursing job at the county hospital, Sophie worked with the reverend's sister, who was also a nurse there.

Although now his affliction was mild and controllable, she was told it hadn't always been that way. In his childhood and teenage years, he had more twitches than a flea-infested cat, but worst of all, they had been accompanied by outbursts of profanity, another symptom of the disorder. Without warning, he would yell out *bitch, dickhead, fuck you*, and other choice words. Thank heavens with treatment, these symptoms were greatly diminished and often disappeared altogether with age. I couldn't help but think, back in the Middle Ages—he wouldn't be teaching God's word; he would have been declared possessed by the devil and burned at the stake! I grimaced thinking about it.

As minister of the United Church for over twenty years, he had presided over many of the town folk's baptisms, weddings, and funerals. However, even with the latest influx of city-weary refugees, the church ranks hadn't grown much. The afterlife wasn't a high priority. People were more interested in the here and now—trying to recapture their youth with face-lifts, Botox and health club memberships.

The church service was drawing to a close, with the choir singing, "A Light Will Shine on You," as the reverend approached the podium.

"I would like to take this opportunity to thank the ladies' auxiliary for all the hard work they did on Friday night's church supper. They did an excellent job raising over two thousand dollars for the church restoration fund." He blinked three times in rapid succession and the corners of his mouth twitched up into a split-second imitation of a smile. "As most of you know, this money is urgently needed for foundation repairs. We have half the five hundred thousand dollars needed, but unfortunately, if we can't come up with the rest soon, we will not only lose our spiritual home, but a beautiful, historic building. This building, the hub of our community, has been used for all kinds of venues: Girl Guides, Scouts, weddings, funerals, political and club meetings, just to name a few. It has withstood the test of time since 1850 and everything Mother-Nature could throw at her. Well, it wasn't Mother Nature, but the county engineers diverting Larson's Creek ten years ago that resulted in the creek running under one corner of the church. The water damage is extensive. So, please give what you can to help shore up the building's foundation. Your generosity is needed now more than ever." Blinking, he twitched a wide grin.

There was twittering throughout the room, with congregants including Sam and I pulling out cheque books.

Reverend Jim's hand went up, shushing everyone. "Before you go, I must draw your attention to the tragic accident that happened outside our church Friday night. I'm sure, by now, most of you have already heard about the hit-and-run death of eight-year-old Trevor Chadwick. We are all deeply saddened. A church fund has been set up for the bereaved family. So, if you can, please help the family out in their time of need. You can donate money or food, or both here at the church. Now, let's bow our heads in prayer."

After the service, the reverend planted himself outside by the front door, shaking hands with his departing flock.

At the top of the stairs, I couldn't help noticing Lara Harding just ahead of us, decked out in a large, black sunhat, black sunglasses, and high heels. A cloud of Chanel No. 5 floated in the air around her. Leaning in, I whispered to Sam, "I guess she doesn't think the 'Fragrance-Free' signs posted everywhere around are meant for her too."

Lara descended the stairs just ahead of us, with Kaydee ahead of her. I could see Lara looking around, surveying the crowd—probably hoping to avoid bumping into any of her husband's employees, who would soon be left jobless when his plant closed. She was so busy looking around that she almost collided with Kaydee, who had stopped dead in her tracks on the step below. A large, ginger cat chased by an even larger tabby took this moment to stand his ground and stopped right in front of Kaydee—hissing, hackles raised, ears back, and teeth bared. Kaydee stood there, hands fluttering about in the air, making high-pitched squeaky sounds.

"Poor girl," I said, turning to Sam. "I didn't know she was *that* afraid of cats!"

After a bit more *cat*erwauling, they finally ran off.

Kaydee took a moment to compose herself, then glanced around to see who had witnessed this unfortunate incident. Facing Lara on the step behind her, she apologized profusely.

This was met with an icy glare and a condescending, "Geez, they're only a couple of damn cats—not bloody African lions!"

Kaydee, cheeks as red as the shoe that had fallen off her foot during the melee, quickly bent over in a dress that was at least a size too small, grabbed the shoe and, wiggling it back on, adjusted her dress, and slunk away.

Lara turned around, shaking her head and rolling her eyes, scanning the faces behind her. Just then her daughter Priscilla came bounding past us and caught up to her mother.

The sole Harding offspring looked more like she was leaving a rave than a solemn church service. Hugging her anorexic frame were jeans with holes in the knees. A short denim jacket that sparkled with sequins over a black tank top completed the ensemble. Her hair, a purple-pink colour combo, was short and gel-spiked—looking like a punk rocker, or some kind of weird exotic bird. However, the eyebrow and nose rings normally worn, were missing today—probably the only concession she'd made to her mother in coming to church this morning.

We met Trish and Georgie waiting at the bottom of the stairs. "I hear you two will be helping out at the Chadwicks' tomorrow," Sam said, looking from one to the other.

Trish sighed, raking her fingers through her short red hair, a silver ring on her finger catching and reflecting the sunlight. "Yes, I'll be going over in the morning to give the kids breakfast and get them off to school. She glanced over at Georgie who was looking around at the dispersing crowd and not paying attention to their conversation. "Georgie will be coming over later to make dinner and put the kids to bed." She shook her head. "I can't imagine what it would be like to lose a child. And I hear Joe hasn't been home since the accident."

Georgie, a June Cleaver look-alike (a character from a TV Land fifties sitcom called *Leave It to Beaver*) was wearing a light-blue cotton, shirt-style dress with pearls and black pumps, finally rejoined the conversation.

"Well, we all know where Joe Chadwick is! Off on another drinking binge. I don't know how that family's going to survive. She glanced over her shoulder, "By the way, has anyone seen where Kaydee went? Did you hear what Lara Harding said to her just now? She can be so mean." Heads nodded in agreement.

"I had no idea Kaydee was that terrified of cats," I said, looking around for her.

"Poor lass," Sophie said, her Scottish brogue evident even after forty years of living in North America. "I knew she had allergies, but didn't know she was catophobic . . ." she shrugged.

Trish looked from Sophie to me. "How did it go for you two last night? Any problems?

"It went well under the circumstances, I said. The kids all ate their dinner. Betty didn't touch her food. Sophie came by later and did the evening shift."

"Such a pity," Sophie said, shaking her head and adjusting the long, silk scarf covered in doggie pictures thrown around her neck. Sophie loved dogs. There was always a picture of a dog or dogs on her clothing. Unfortunately for Sophie, she was dog-less at the moment, since her beloved Bichon, Snowball, got carted off by a coyote last winter while out taking a pee in the backyard. Poor Sophie had witnessed the whole thing from her kitchen window and had raced out into the snow in her nightgown and slippers and chased after the coyote until it disappeared with little Snowball in its jaws.

Edda came over and joined our group. Sam turned to her, "I hear your menfolk are away attending a conference. How are you managing by yourself?"

"Fine, but I'll be glad when they're back home on Wednesday night. Just then Lara Harding—nudging her daughter along—passed by.

Someone asked Sam a question, diverting his attention away momentarily. I quickly pulled Edda aside and, lowering my voice, asked, "Have you told the police chief about the logo yet?"

Edda glanced quickly at me, then looked away. "Not yet."

I looked at her, puzzled, but before I could say anything else, we heard loud laughter coming from the other side of the parking lot. Looking over, I saw Lara and Prissy Harding leaning against Lara's light-grey Mercedes, engaged in a humorous conversation with another couple. I had noticed Seymour Harding wasn't at church today. Keeping a low profile, I figured. Besides, on such a beautiful day, I was sure golf was calling to him more than the Almighty.

Edda nibbled on her bottom lip. "I guess I was wrong about Seymour." She looked at me. "Brynn, would you come to the police station with me tomorrow?"

"Yes, of course I will . . ." I hesitated, rubbing my chin, thinking. "Would you feel better if we paid Seymour a visit first to see what he has to say?"

Edda seemed relieved at this suggestion, and nodded.

"I can get away from the shop around noon tomorrow. How about I pick you up, and we'll drive out to the meat plant together." Our eyes locked for a split second before we turned back to the rest of the group.

CHAPTER SIX

Lara

(Monday, June 11)

LARA DRAGGED HERSELF OUT of bed to make breakfast for her family, who didn't seem to appreciate her efforts. Her husband's eggs and toast were getting cold as he sipped his coffee, his nose buried in the newspaper. Prissy hadn't even bothered getting out of bed yet. The shower upstairs was silent. She should have showered, dressed, and finished fussing with her hair and makeup by now. It was eight o'clock.

Lara stomped to the bottom of the stairs and yelled up. After hearing a loud groan and satisfied that life was stirring above, she went back to the kitchen and put more bread in the toaster. "Your daughter's going to be late for school—again!" She eyed Seymour, who, engrossed in the financial section of the paper, ignored her.

The top-of-the-hour news came on the radio. The lead story was the hit-and-run accident on Friday night.

Seymour lowered his paper and looked over the top of his reading glasses perched on the tip of his nose. "That was terrible what happened to the Chadwick boy. The police are asking anyone who saw a young boy riding a blue bike through town Friday night, or anyone who may have dashcam footage of the area, to contact them. I hear the accident happened right in front of the church. Apparently the women cleaning up after the church dinner witnessed it."

Lara looked at him, shrugged, then opened the fridge door and got out the orange juice carton. "Well, I'm not surprised by what happened. Those Chadwick kids run wild. They are out at all hours of the day and night. Something was bound to happen to one of them." She took the carton to the table and filled the three small juice glasses. "And what I don't understand is why people like that have so many kids to begin with, when they can barely afford to feed themselves. Well, at least now there's one less mouth to feed." She saw Seymour roll his eyes, fold his newspaper over to the next page, ignoring her, and continue reading.

Prissy trudged into the kitchen dressed in faded jeans, a pink Gap T-shirt and an oversized white cardigan. She was also wearing her full complement of hardware: eyebrow and nose rings, multiple ear piercings, and her latest addition, not visible, a tongue stud. Lara prayed her daughter would outgrow this hardware stage soon, but she wasn't counting on it, for like her daughter's attitude, the hardware was entrenched. Dropping her backpack on the floor, Prissy sank onto a chair and pulled the sweater sleeves down over her hands, folding her arms across her body like she was wearing a straitjacket. She was always cold, no matter what the temperature was outside. It could be 150 degrees in the shade but, still not warm enough for her. Her body was a twig, without an ounce of fat—no insulation—probably the reason she couldn't get warm.

Lara shook her head in frustration as she watched her daughter push the eggs around her plate. Picking up the empty juice carton and other recyclables off the counter, she walked through the connecting door off the kitchen to the recycle bins out in the garage. She flipped on the light and headed over to the bins. Her heart stopped when she saw the Lincoln's front bumper bashed in, with what looked like mud or dried bloodstains on it.

With her heart pounding, she returned to the kitchen and threw her daughter a stone-cold glare. Then, snatching up the coffee-pot, she made her way over to refill Seymour's cup. She wondered if he could see the vein pulsating in her neck.

"Is everything okay?" he asked, holding up his cup.

"Fine," she said, massaging her temples. "Just a bit of a headache."

Prissy lay sprawled out on the table. Her head rested in the crook of one arm, eyes closed, while the other arm struggled to hold her cup up—like a man dying of thirst in the desert.

Her mother wacked her across the back of the head. "Sit up straight and have some toast. Eat *something* for Christ's sake!"

Prissy, half expecting another swat, cringed down, her arm covering her head, and whined, "*Mom*!"

They were just finishing breakfast when a horn blared from the driveway. Mrs. Hicks and her daughter Tara were here to pick Prissy up for school. The teen pushed back her chair, and grabbing her backpack, she mumbled, "Later," and headed for the front door.

"Prissy, wait." Lara called after her, grabbing her purse and fishing around inside, then hurried after her, waving a twenty-dollar bill in the air. "Don't forget your lunch money."

When she caught up with her daughter in the hall, she grabbed her roughly by the arm and yanked her closer.

"Pris, you took your dad's car out last night!" She said, through teeth clenched tighter than a Scotsman's wallet. "Where the hell did you go, and what the hell did you hit?"

"Whaa? Tara couldn't pick me up, so I drove myself over to her place. I didn't hit anything, honest Mum," she lisped, her tongue still swollen from the new piercing. I haven't a clue whaa happened to Dad's car. Maybe when I was parked at the variety store to buy cigs, someone hit me or something—I dunno." The car horn beeped again from the driveway. "I gotta go, they're waitin' for me." She pulled herself free of her mother's grasp, snatched the twenty-dollar bill, and flew out the door.

Lara's gaze hardened as she watched her daughter go. Then she headed back into the kitchen, her mind spinning—trying to think of an excuse for the car damage she could tell her husband before he saw it.

"You give that girl way too much money," he scowled, watching as she came back into the kitchen and collapsed into her chair at the table.

"Kids need more money these days compared to when we were young. Everything costs so much. You didn't mind spending a whack of money on your bloody golf outing this weekend at that fancy golf resort. But for God's sake Morty, you begrudge your only daughter a few bucks?"

Seymour sat there shaking his head.

"By the way," Lara said as she got up and carried the dishes over to the kitchen sink. "When you were away, my car wouldn't start. I used the Lincoln to go to my bridge game in Beckford on Friday night. It was foggy when I headed home. A deer ran out of the woods right in front of me—no warning at all! I hit it. I've noticed the 'deer hazards' warning signs his time of year, so I was cautious. But with the fog Friday night—all I can say is thank God for seat belts! Didn't kill the damn thing though. Saw it hobble off into the woods. Probably dead by now." She paused. "It did a pretty good job on the front of your car though."

"Geez, Lara! And you're just telling me this now?" His brows knit together, eyes narrowing as he stared at his wife. "You're sure it was a deer you hit?"

"What do you mean? Do you think I don't know a deer when I see one?"

Seymour stared at her in disbelief. "Lara, your car has been running just fine, and you drove it to church yesterday, didn't you?"

"Well, yes, but for some reason it wouldn't start Friday night and I didn't want to be late for bridge, so I took yours. I tried my car again yesterday morning, and after a few tries, I was surprised it started."

Glancing at his watch, Seymour stood up abruptly. "We'd better get going. I have a friend who owns a body shop over in Grimley. We'll drive both cars over there, and I'll have them take a look at your car as well—probably just a loose wire, and then you can drive me to work."

Lara followed Seymour out to the garage. He walked over to inspect the damage to his car. She couldn't help wincing when she saw him do a double-take as he noticed the blue scuff marks and scratches embedded in the paint.

On the drive to school, Prissy saw Dylan walking along the sidewalk in town. She asked her friend's mom to slow down, then opened the window and leaning out, yelled, "Hey Dylan!"

He kept walking.

Wearing earphones, he probably hadn't heard her. She yelled louder, "Hey freak!"

This time, he stopped, pulled his earphones out, and, seeing her hanging out the car window, headed over. He accepted their lift offer and climbed in the back seat next to Prissy. She snuggled close, lifting his jean jacket. "I know what you got under there," she said whispering. "Friday night was, like . . . amazing."

His face cracked a smile as he leaned over and kissed her.

CHAPTER SEVEN

Brynn

(Monday, June 11)

EDDA AND I PULLED into the parking lot of the grey, two-story concrete factory building. A large aluminium sign over the front door proclaimed in big, bold red lettering—Harding Meat Packers.

The company employed about a hundred full and part-time staff. It was one of the three big employers in the county. Other than farming or the tourist trade, residents in this small community worked either at the Harding Meat Plant, the Hillcrest Mushroom Farm or Blatt's Canning Factory. Unfortunately, when the meat plant closed its doors, many families would suffer. Seymour made it clear the current employees were not welcome at the new plant being constructed three hours east of Hubbs Harbour.

It was now lunch-time, and the parking lot usually full, had a few empty spaces. After finding a spot, I switched off the engine and we sat there. Our eyes converged on the empty parking space marked "CEO," where the Harding's Lincoln Town Car normally parked.

Leaning back, Edda sighed, "Maybe he's not in today."

I looked over at her. "I think it's more likely his car is at the garage getting repaired." I put my hand on the door handle... "Come on, let's get this over with."

We walked into the building and up to the reception desk. Behind the desk was a good-looking twentyish, platinum blonde with cleavage Pamela Anderson would envy. Her name tag read "Bunny Benoit." After asking to see Seymour and giving our names, the receptionist picked up the phone and dialed his office.

"He's on his lunch break," she said, batting her long fake eyelashes at us. "But he says it's okay for you to go on up. Just take the elevator to the second floor, turn right, and it's the big office at the end of the hall."

The door was open as we approached his office. We could see Seymour sitting behind his desk, eating his lunch. When he saw us, he put down his sandwich, stood up and, wiping his mouth with a napkin, waved us in.

"Please come in. It's nice to see you ladies."

I managed a nervous smile. "Sorry to bother you at lunchtime, Seymour," I said, reaching behind me and grasping the doorknob. "Do you mind if I close the door? This is a rather personal matter."

"No... no bother at all, please by all means." He came around from behind his desk fastening the bottom button of his jacket. "I keep the door open for better air circulation. I can guess why you ladies are here. Please sit down and make yourself comfortable." He pointed to the two grey leather tub chairs sitting in front of his desk.

We remained standing.

"Would you ladies like a coffee?" he asked, then headed over to the coffeepot sitting on the credenza under the large picture window overlooking the plant floor below. Picking up the coffeepot, he glanced over at Edda. "I hear your menfolk are away. Lara mentioned overhearing you say they were away attending a conference. How are you managing at the farm all on your own?"

Edda, finding it hard to look him in the eyes, glanced down at her feet. "Do'in just fine. I'm managing with help from our farmhand Ben."

"That's good to hear." About to pour the coffee, he asked, "What would you ladies like in your coffee?"

"No coffee for us thanks" I answered. "We'd like to get straight to the point of our visit."

"Yes, of course." He poured one for himself and again gestured for us to take a seat.

Again, we ignored his offer and continued standing.

"I guess I've been a little stingy on my contribution to the church restoration fund. I think I can manage a few more dollars," he said, going back to his desk and opening the top drawer. He got out a chequebook, picked up a pen, and was about to start writing.

"It's not about that at all, Seymour. It's about Friday night, the hit-and-run accident out front of the church. We were there, the ladies' auxiliary, cleaning up after the dinner." I paused for a second, then— "Edda witnessed the whole thing from the kitchen window."

Seymour tilted his head to one side, eyebrows lifting. "Yes, that was a terrible thing that happened."

Edda's eyes darted to mine before she spoke.

I nodded.

"I saw your car, Seymour. It was your car that hit that boy on the bike—and you didn't even stop! You just kept going!"

The pleasantness melted from his face, faster than a snow cone dropped in hell. At a loss for words, all he could manage was, "Huh?"

"It was your car, Seymour. I recognized the logo on the door," Edda continued.

He took a step back. "What the hell are you talking about? I wasn't even in town Friday night! I was nowhere near there." His face scrunched up in bewilderment as he leaned against the desk, his mouth hanging open. He paused. "If that's what you think you saw, why haven't you gone to the police? It's obvious you haven't or I would have heard from them by now."

"I only remembered seeing the logo on the car *after* speaking with the police," Edda said. "We thought you would have gone to the police yourself by now. We're amazed you haven't—after all—it was an accident!"

Seymour undid the button he had just done up a moment ago and slowly lowered himself down into his chair. His eyes needled us suspiciously, his lips a straight, tight line. As his backside hit the seat, his face suddenly morphed into a wicked smile.

"Okay, now I get it— *how much money do you want?*"

Time seemed to stand still as I turned and stared at Edda. This was the last thing we had expected to hear from him. I opened my mouth to speak but was at a loss for words.

Finally, I got my voice back. "What? You're offering us money? Good God, Seymour, do you think we're black-mailing you?"

"Well, you're here aren't you, and not at the police station? I think that pretty much answers the question."

Just as I was about to speak, Seymour cut me off…

"I told you I was out of town—all weekend. I was golfing with my friends. Yes, my car was at home, but no one drives that car but me. Lara has her own car and Prissy sure as hell wouldn't have taken it."

He closed his eyes, shaking his head, then opening them, he looked at us. His face strained. "You are badly mistaken—but even if a hint of this gets out involving me, it will ruin my reputation. And I don't want the police drawn into this." His eyes flitted back and forth between Edda and me. "So, how much money do you want—to keep quiet about what you *think* you saw?"

I was so stunned, I just stood there staring at him like he had two heads.

He picked the pen up off his desk and began writing in his chequebook. Then, reaching his arm out across the desk, he shoved the cheque towards me. "I'm sure this is more than enough money to help out the Chadwick family; God knows they need it, and part of the money can go toward the church foundation work."

Ignoring the cheque, I said, "We don't want—"

"Please," he pleaded, continuing to push the cheque at me.

When I wouldn't take it, he finally dropped his arm. "Just think about it. It wasn't my car. But even if it was, what good would come from involving the police *now* do? It's only your word against mine."

He sat back down, looking quite small behind the large mahogany desk. As he loosened the knot in his tie, I could see beads of sweat forming on his forehead. "Yes, it was a horrible accident, but why not have something positive come from it—financial help for the Chadwick family, and the church certainly needs the money." He looked up as if seeking help from a higher source before looking back down at us.

"The only thing is—I don't want anyone to know where this *donation* came from, not the church, the Chadwicks, especially not my wife. That's all I ask."

Just then there was a knock on the door and the blonde head of the receptionist poked in. "Sorry to bother you, Morty, I, um, mean Mr. Harding," she said, stealing a look in our direction. "We're having trouble with the deboning machine in the plant again. Jack Saunders almost lost his hand trying to get that thing started, and now it's stopped again."

Seymour stood up. "I'm coming," he said, readjusting his tie. His eyes fell on us. "Don't be too hasty turning down my offer. It makes sense. Then, before I could object, he shoved the cheque into my hand—and dashed from the room.

CHAPTER EIGHT

Brynn

(Tuesday June 12)

I TOSSED AND TURNED all night, a nightmare marathon of distressing thoughts playing out in my head. I knew what we should do—go to the police! That's what Sam would say without hesitation; his no-nonsense honesty is one of the reasons I loved him so much. But not everything is black and white, and sometimes doing the *right* thing isn't always the *best* thing.

My heart broke every time I thought of that little girl's disfigured face. Although my situation hadn't been anywhere near as dire as Deedee's, when I was a kid, I knew only too well how nasty other kids could be. In kindergarten, I'd started wearing horn-rimmed glasses—Coke-bottle-thick—to correct my crossed eyes. It gave me a distorted, bug-eyed look. To make matters worse, the bulky frames were so heavy, when I looked down, they kept falling off my nose. So, to keep them in place, I had to wear a strap that went around the back of my head and hooked onto the arms. I had to put up with the name-calling—*Alien,*

Specky-four-eyes, *Bugsy*, and other creepy names. I'd had no friends, except for Ziggy, a boy with autism who had been called names too.

My father committed suicide when I was six. And, if it wasn't for the help of the church, I'm not sure how our family would have ever survived. They counselled my mother and brought her back from her deep depression. And, they made sure my brother and I had everything we needed, including funding for my eye surgery at age eight.

Didn't it make more sense to help little Deedee and her poverty-stricken family and save the church from crumbling to the ground, than putting Seymour behind bars? Seymour's money could make a grave (no pun intended) situation better.

And what good would putting Seymour behind bars do? It had been an accident. In the fog Friday night, anyone could have hit that boy. And we weren't blackmailing Seymour, he *offered* us the money—a donation. A sizeable one at that—half a million dollars! Shouldn't we use it for something good? Maybe it was worth the lapse in memory?

I checked the clock on the nightstand—2:00 a.m. As I didn't want to wake Sam with my tossing and turning, I begrudgingly left our warm, cozy nest to go to the cold, empty bed in the spare bedroom. Chewie jumped down and followed me. I was surprised when the next time I looked at the clock it was 5:30.

Pulling on my housecoat, I went downstairs, Chewy close on my heels. After letting him out to do his business, I put the coffee on. When it was ready, I grabbed my mug and headed for the sunroom, where I made myself comfortable and admired the amazing sunrise over the water. It appeared as if God had dipped His paintbrush into a palette of pastel shades— streaks of beach-glass blue, watermelon pink, lavender, and pale gold brushed across the sky. With my hands wrapped around my oversized "Reading Is Sexy" mug, I soaked in the awe-inspiring beauty and serenity of the moment, knowing full well the turmoil that this afternoon's meeting would bring.

Taking a sip, I thought of happier times, like when Sam and I first moved out to the county. We knew the area well from visiting my brother and his family and had fallen in love with it. So, when my brother told Sam about a job opening with the municipality for a town planner, he applied and, surprise, got the job! I'd been working at the Fairfield Health Clinic, in Toronto, as a dietician, counselling patients with diabetes and eating disorders. But, with my depression after my miscarriages, I was finding it hard to cope and having people's health depending on me was too stressful. I needed a change. After moving to the county, the little health food shop in Penrith came up for sale, and I jumped at the chance to buy it.

We got our "kid fix" by spoiling rotten and babysitting my niece and nephew. Finally, we decided to take the big step and adopt.

It was love at first sight! The little mop-topped Morkie at the pound grabbed our hearts right away. We named him Chewie after the furry Wookiee of Star Wars fame *Chewbacca*. We found out the name fit in more ways than one after the first time we left him home alone. We returned to find the house littered with mangled shoes, holey carpets and teeth marks in the baseboards—as if a deranged beaver had visited and gone on a rampage!

I heard Sam stirring on the floor above me, and my mind quickly swung back to the present. It was now six-thirty. I made more coffee and took a couple of our pantry's breakfast sandwiches out of the freezer. Once again, my mind returned to this afternoon's meeting…wondering how the women would react to Seymour's *donation*? Would they object to keeping his secret?

I jumped when Sam came up behind me in the kitchen.

"A penny for your thoughts," he said, bending over and kissing my neck.

I looked at him. "Is that all they're worth? With inflation, I'd think they're worth at least a buck by now."

He smiled, his dimples lighting up his whole face, and gave me another kiss.

While I waited for the microwave to beep, Sam poured himself a coffee and sat down at the table. I watched him, a puppy love smile stuck on my face. Dressed for work, he looked like a model for a business ad—crisp white shirt, purple tie, and grey/blue suit jacket tossed over the corner of the chair. I loved this man, not only for his great looks, but for the honest, gentle beauty that came from deep within.

I knew the women had arrived even before the doorbell rang, with Chewie's constant yapping and jumping around with excitement. I slid my banana loaf out of the oven and set it on the stovetop, then hurried towards the door, almost tripping over the dog running back and forth in front of me. I gave the hand signal to sit and was surprised when he actually did! Unfortunately, it only lasted for a few seconds until the door opened.

Edda was first through the door and stepped aside, letting the other women file past her. They greeted me and fussed over the dog.

SILENCE IS ~~GOLDEN~~ DEADLY

Once they had all passed by, Edda nodded toward the open door and Joe Chadwick puttering about outside on the front lawn. "So, Joe Chadwick is working here now, Brynn?"

With a nod, I closed the door. "I saw him slumped over on a park bench yesterday as if he'd spent the night there. His clothes were a mess and he looked like he hadn't shaved in a while. He's probably feeling guilty about his son's death—coming home drunk that night and all. I couldn't help but feel sorry for him. I knew he wouldn't accept a handout, so I offered him a job doing yard work. It will help keep his mind busy while giving him a few bucks. God knows, he needs the money. Unfortunately, we can guess where it will end up." I shrugged.

The ladies were all settled comfortably in the living room when I noticed that Kaydee was missing from the group. I went back and poked my head out the front door. I still didn't see her, so I stepped out onto the porch. There she was, standing on the sidewalk, her naturally blonde hair pulled back in a tight ponytail with a small red scarf tied under her chin. It did nothing to lessen the fullness of her face. Her head seemed small compared to the copious body below hidden under a long, billowy sundress. I couldn't help thinking she looked like a Russian Babushka doll, with smaller versions of herself nesting one inside the other.

Staring up at the porch steps, she didn't move.

"Are you coming in, Kaydee?" I called out, wondering why she wasn't moving. Then looking down, I noticed what all the fuss was about—our neighbor's black cat Kiki was lying on the bottom porch step in the sun grooming himself. After the church incident, and knowing how frightened Kaydee was of cats, I quickly shooed it away.

She held her hand over her heart, looking relieved, and schlepped her way up the steps toward me. After thanking me for rescuing her, she put her tote bag and shoes in the hallway along with the others, then joined the women in the living room while I headed back to the kitchen.

I brought out the tea, coffee, and cake and set them on the dining table; I had set out the cups, saucers, plates, and napkins earlier. The women helped themselves, taking their refreshments back into the living room and making themselves comfortable.

Chewie ran around excitedly greeting one person then another as if this gathering was arranged just for him. Kaydee, sitting uncomfortably with her knees pressed tightly together, looked uneasy as the dog came up to her wagging his tail. I was just about to grab him and put him in another room, when Sophie called the dog over, gave him a doggie biscuit and told him to lie down.

Sophie always carried doggie treats with her. They were hidden in every nook and cranny on her person, and she pulled them out magically when needed, like a magician pulling cards out of a hat. The dog obeyed without hesitation and lay down quietly at Sophie's feet. Today Sophie was wearing her handmade, quilted doggy-print vest, covered with every size, shape, and breed of canine imaginable.

Turning my attention back to the uneasy task at hand, I stood up and, clearing my throat, tapped my spoon against my cup to get everyone's attention. "I'd like to get right to the point of this meeting. The twittering subsided and they all looked at me. "I'm not sure how to begin, but I'll try." I cleared my throat again. "A rather unusual situation has come up."

I began recounting the events that happened after Edda and I left the other women the night of the accident and how Edda had remembered seeing and recognizing a logo on the hit-and-run vehicle's door. Just then, I heard the clicking sound of garden shears coming from the open dining room window and turned in time to see Joe Chadwick's head disappear behind the leafy bushes he was trimming. I went over and closed the window. Returning, I continued on with events leading up to the present. All was deathly quiet, except for the occasional gasp of "Oh, my God!" Then, I fished in my jean's pocket and pulled out the cheque.

It was so quiet you could almost hear the hearts pounding in the room. Kaydee looked around the room, her brows forming a deep V—"Well, I don't understand what you're waiting for… go to the police!"

"Not so fast. I can understand why Brynn and Edda haven't gone to the police yet and have kept the cheque," said Sophie. "Think about it for a moment. This money could be a godsend for the Chadwicks, and the poor wee lassie could have the surgery she needs. She could lead a normal life."

"I agree with Sophie," Trish said, straightening up in her chair. "Trevor's gone, but his family still needs help. We should think of what's best for the living now."

The only one who hadn't spoken yet was Georgie.

She patted her coiffed hair before fidgeting with the pearl necklace around her throat, her manicured nails shiny-pink with polish. "Well, I don't know. It seems wrong to me to just let Seymour Harding get away with this. He left the scene of the accident, and he killed a boy!"

Edda spoke up. "Yes, but it was an accident. He's not really getting away with anything as far as I can see. He has to live with what he's done, and unless he confesses and gets it off his chest, it will eat at him his entire life."

I looked around. "For the last three years our church group has voted on all decisions, big and small. We've considered them all carefully. This will be the biggest decision we'll ever make—people's lives will be greatly affected by it. So, what's the right course of action?" Leaning back on the couch, I folded my arms across my chest, scanning the room.

Kaydee squirmed in her chair. "Sounds like we're playing God to me."

I stared at her, then my eyes drifted around the room. "Let's pray we make the right decision."

The ladies looked at one another, some nodding their agreement, others shaking their heads in doubt. The room fell quiet again; even the hum of the lawnmower in the back yard had stopped. Snoozing on top of Sophie's feet, Chewie didn't seem to have care in the world.

My eyes shifted to Edda and back. "Edda and I have thought about Seymour's offer a great deal, and we both feel it would be best to keep the money—give half to the church and half to the Chadwick family. Anyone else agree with us?"

"Aye," said Sophie.

Trish nodded. "It can make the best of a tragic situation."

"I'm not sure," said Georgie hesitating, "but I guess so."

All eyes now focused on Kaydee. "Can't we have more time to think about this? How can you make such a big decision on the spot? I'd at least like to go home and sleep on it." Then she mumbled to herself, "*I probably won't be able to sleep again ever!*"

"We need to know where you stand now," I said, with a sigh. "You're right about this being a monumental decision. People's lives are depending on it. So, the sooner we make the decision the better."

Kaydee slumped back in her seat, head down, then looked up, scanning all the faces looking at her. "Okay," she finally said. Take the money."

CHAPTER NINE

Brynn

(Wednesday, June 13)

SOPHIE AND I ARRANGED to meet with Reverend Jim at the church a few minutes before the monthly 10:00 a.m. council meeting. He ushered us into a small anteroom off the main meeting room and closed the ornate oak door with the carved wooden cross on the front.

Twitching, he blinked three times, his tics getting the better of him. "Now ladies what can I do for you?"

I glanced at Sophie, then pulled Seymour's cheque out of my purse and handed it to him. "We're pleased to pass this donation on to the church. As you can see, it's from an anonymous donor. He, or she, stipulates that half the money is to go to the church restoration fund and the other half to the Chadwick family—a portion of that money being earmarked for Deedee's reconstructive surgery."

As the reverend glanced at the cheque, his eyebrows shot skyward, eyes wide. "Half a million dollars! Oh, my Lord," he said, looking back at us. "This *is* a large sum of money; how wonderful. Our prayers have been answered!" His face lit up. We can begin the foundation repair right away. He looked at the cheque again, to make sure it was real, then looked back at me. "I must call the donor and thank him *or her* personally, and of course, I'll make sure he, *or she*, gets a tax receipt."

"Actually," I said, "you will notice the cheque is written on a trust account. The donor's name doesn't appear anywhere on it; they insist on remaining anonymous. No acknowledgment, no call, no letter, no anything."

He stared at me over the top of the glasses sitting on the end of his nose. Then, shoving them back up with his middle finger, he continued to stare, first at me, then at Sophie. "Surely this person would at least want a tax credit for donating this amount of money!"

I shook my head, wanting to believe this money was a donation but, knowing full-well, it was really hush money. Seymour didn't want a paper trail.

Reverend Jim continued to stare at the both of us blinking and twitching. "Not even a tax receipt?"

"That's right," I said.

Finally, he shrugged his shoulders. "Well, if that's what the donor wants, who am I to argue with such a selfless act? The Lord certainly works in mysterious ways." He glanced at the clock above the door. "The council meeting is just about to get started, so we better go in."

After locking the cheque in his desk, he led us into the meeting room grinning from ear to ear. With palms pressed together in payer, he raised his hands high in the air and announced—"Praise be to the Lord. A miracle has occurred!" And this time, along with his twitching, he gave a loud *whoop*!

Our bodies suddenly tensed when we saw who was sitting at the conference table. Seymour! We hadn't expected him to be here. He didn't usually attend the monthly meetings. He glanced up at us, and if looks could kill—

CHAPTER TEN

Edda

(Wednesday, June 13)

EDDA MADE A FRIED-EGG sandwich for dinner. She wasn't hungry, and besides, she didn't like cooking for just one. Dinner was usually a boisterous family affair, with heaps of food on the table and gargantuan appetites to match. This sandwich would be her last meal alone, before Henk and the boys returned home later that evening. Her mouth curved into a smile knowing how eager they would be to share all the latest dairy farming news with her. She had wanted to go along, but someone had to stay behind and mind the farm—the cows couldn't milk themselves, and she'd wanted her "men" to go to the conference together. Her smile faded at the thought of her own news—the tragic hit-and-run death of the Chadwick boy.

She washed the sandwich down with an icy-cold glass of farm fresh milk and looked up at the kitchen clock; it was almost 6:00 p.m.

The sun was still up as she ambled down the dusty dirt lane towards the pasture. The gentle breeze tussled her hair, carrying with it the sweet scent of the alfalfa fields along with the occasional, not so sweet, scent of chicken manure covering the cornfields. Seeing the tractor sitting off in the field brought back memories. It was about four months after she had first met Henk at a church outing when his father died in a freak farm accident. He had been out harvesting hay when a huge bale slid off the frontend loader and fell onto the open tractor cab. Henk found his father out in the field five hours later, crushed, pinned in his seat. Henk was only twenty-four at the time.

After his father's death, Henk, with the help of a hired hand, helped his mother run the farm, and he still managed to get his college degree. Unfortunately, a year later, his mother suffered a stroke, leaving him to manage the farm on his own. Two months later, he and Edda were married. They combined their farming knowledge, modernized operations, and established a successful farming operation. They raised two sons, Derek and Karl—the "boys," now in their twenties, who pitched in on the farm when not away at school.

As Edda approached the pasture, the cows lifted their heads in unison, their big, brown bovine eyes watching her as she approached the low electrified wire fence. They began shifting around and mooing in anticipation of their evening meal. When she reached the metal gate, she gave it a good shake before opening it. The clanging was a signal to the girls that it was dinner time. The cows meandered over, passed through the gate, and formed a long conga line following the path up to the paddock. Once they were all in the enclosure, Edda opened another gate, allowing sixteen cows at a time to make their way single file up the ramp along the concrete platform and into the milking station. Then she guided each animal into a milking bay, eight bays per side. The cows went willingly, eager to get to their mixed rations of barley, oats and alfalfa.

After pulling a lever and locking the cows in place, she rushed around giving their udders a quick wipe-down with disinfectant before attaching the milking apparatus and turning the machine on. With the mechanical hum as a backdrop, the cows settled into the familiar routine of eating and chewing their cud.

Her thoughts turned to the farm open house coming up in a couple of weeks. It was held once a year. It gave the public a chance to visit the area farms and see where their food actually came from. It didn't just appear magically on supermarket shelves. Edda always enjoyed people visiting their farm. They were always impressed with her cow knowledge. One black and white cow looked the same as the next to most folks, but Edda could tell them apart. She named all seventy cows on the farm and knew them by sight. A Holstein's spots were like fingerprints, she would tell people—no two exactly alike. Besides their markings, each cow's size and weight helped distinguish them, and if that failed, Edda could always cheat by checking their ear tags.

"Cows have personalities too," she would tell her visitors, raising a few eyebrows. "Like Lulubelle here," she'd say, pointing out a favourite cow. She was named Lulubelle III, after the cow pictured on the cover of Pink Floyd's 1970's hit album, *Atom Heart Mother*. (She and Henk had piles of old record albums, left to them by Henk's dad, and this was one of their favourite*s*). She'd tell them how Lulu liked to be first in line to the milking parlour, while other cows were content to just lag along behind her. Some cows were aggressive and moody, like Pauline, the Hendriks' prize-winning cow named after Pauline Wayne, pet cow to U.S. President Taft. When the president's cow first arrived at the White House in 1910, she'd made the front page of *The New York*

Times. She had grazed on the White House lawn and provided fresh milk and butter to the First Family.

Edda would show visitors through their modern free-stall barn—just as the name implies—it allowed the cows to move around freely inside the barn. Some liked the warm sunny side, while others preferred the cool shady side.

She would tell visitors that the dairy business was a 24/7, 365 days a year job—but she loved it. She was raised on a dairy farm and her grandparents had been dairy farmers back in Holland before emigrating to Canada.

Edda was busy hooking up the next lot of cows to the milking machine when she thought she heard a noise coming from the far end of the barn. She stopped, straining to hear. Maybe, she thought, smiling, her husband Henk and the boys were home early. Hearing nothing else, she shrugged and went back to work.

Again, she heard something—this time it was a loud humming sound coming from the back of the barn. She straightened up, hands rubbing her lower back, a puzzled look on her face. Maybe their hired hand Ben had arrived.

"Ben, that you?" She called.

Evening shadows crept across the barn, but no one answered. She crossed her arms, tilting her head to one side listening. All was silent again, except for the cows shifting their feet and swishing their tails about restlessly. She figured she'd quickly finish hooking up this group of cows, then go check it out.

A short while later, she felt a tickle in her throat and began coughing. Then, crinkling her nose rabbit-like, she sniffed at the air. Detecting a rotten egg odor, she knew immediately this wasn't a good sign.

"Ben?" she shouted, louder this time. Pulling a handkerchief out of her back pocket, she held it over her nose and mouth, and crouching down between the metal safety bars at the end of the milking platform, lowered herself to the barn floor, three feet below. A loud clang echoed through the barn startling her, and she hurried off in the direction of the noise. It seemed to be coming from the pump room located just above the sub-floor storage tank at the far end of the barn. The large underground tank held the effluent and solid waste that was hosed down daily through the slotted concrete barn floor above.

The cows, more agitated now began shifting around and mooing. Edda's coughing increased the closer she got to the source of the noise. The smell,stronger now, was making her nauseous.

She noticed the trap door to the underground sewage tank was wide open. Someone was down there. Looking down, she was surprised to see Ben—covered from head to toe, in a yellow hazmat suit, with breathing apparatus—pumping out the manure sludge.

She realized how dangerous the hydrogen sulphide and methane gasses being released into the air by the agitation were. The sewage tank was due to be pumped out in the next couple of weeks—but not now, and *not* when there were people and animals in the barn, with no safety precautions in place! Oh, my God, what was he thinking?

Bending over the railing, she wildly waved her hanky in the air to get his attention. "Hey, Ben! What the hell are you doing . . . Ben?"

Although she couldn't see the face hidden beneath the breathing apparatus, she realized it wasn't Ben. Ben was tall, with broad shoulders—built like a fridge—while this person was smaller and slight of build.

Ignoring her, the yellow-suited figure continued gripping the hose and kept on agitating and pumping the sludge.

Edda clomped down the four steps into the pump room, her breathing heavy. She felt sick to her stomach, and a minute later, she bent over and threw up. With her stomach churning and lungs burning, she grabbed at the yellow-suited figure and was viciously shoved aside. She stumbled, almost falling, unaware of the heavy metal hose-end being swung at the back of her head. It came whacking down, knocking her to the concrete floor. Lying there dazed, she struggled to get up just as another crushing blow struck her head. She lay there, blood now gushing down her face, blurring her eyes from the wide-open gash on her head. Finally, managing to lift her head, her eyes came into focus on the gas detection monitor on the opposite wall. The reading was off the chart! She knew she had only minutes . . .

She struggled to her hands and knees, gasping, then slowly dragged her body up the steps. At the top, she could just make out the yellow-suited figure gimping out of the barn. Flicking what looked like a lit cigarette back inside.

CHAPTER ELEVEN

Brynn

(Evening, June 13)

I WAS ONCE AGAIN lending a hand over at the Chadwicks' house. Betty's depression hadn't lifted, making it difficult for her to focus on the kids and household tasks, and Joe still hadn't come home.

After making dinner and washing up, I sank onto a chair at the kitchen table, sipping a glass of water and waited for Sophie's arrival. She worked part-time at the meat packing plant during the day, so the evening shift at the Chadwicks was best for her. Money was tight for Sophie and her husband. Her nursing pension was small, and her husband's workman's compensation ran out years ago. Before his back injury, he worked at the canning factory. It was lifting all those heavy boxes that did it. Sophie was glad to have any job at her age, especially a part-time job where she could pick her own hours. This gave her time to tend to her ailing husband. Now, with the plant closing, that extra money would be sorely missed.

I looked in at Betty slumped in the living room rocker, eyes closed, chair gently creaking back and forth—back and forth. She had only picked at her dinner. The children had eaten well and were once again gathered on the carpet in front of the TV. This time *Sponge Bob Square Pants* captured their attention. Baby Arti was asleep in his bassinet. Dylan was up in his room and hadn't bothered coming down for dinner.

My phone rang. I pulled it from my pants pocket. It was Sam.

"Hi Honey," I said, glad to hear his voice.

"Brynn, I . . . He was having a hard time catching his breath, as if he'd been running a marathon.

"What . . . is everything okay?"

"No, something terrible has happened! There was a huge explosion and fire at the Hendriks' barn." Silence for a moment. "Then . . . the police think Edda was in the barn."

I stood rooted in place, my eyes huge in disbelief. I had to tell myself to breathe. "No! Oh, my God! This can't be happening. When? How? They only *think* she was in the barn, right? They must be a mistaken."

Just then, there was a knock at the front door. I glanced over as the door opened and Sophie let herself in.

I spoke back into the phone. "Maybe she wasn't home. Maybe she was out doing errands. That's possible? What do you mean by an explosion? What kind of an explosion?"

"It's too soon to tell, Hon. It just happened. Everyone's out at the Hendriks' place now. Firefighters from all over the region are helping our guys. The police, ambulances, and even Animal Control are here. Sweetie, since I'm part of the Emergency Relief Task Force, I've gotta go. I'll let you know more when I hear anything. Are you okay?"

"I guess... Sophie's just arrived. Call me back as soon as you can, and Sam, be careful!"

"You know I will. Love you."

I put the phone down and stared at Sophie, who looked grief-stricken, her eyes brimming with tears. She had heard the news on the radio on the way over.

We stood there, dumbstruck. Then Sophie came over and wrapped her bird-thin arms around me. We stayed intertwined for what seemed like forever before I finally pulled away.

"Soph, I can't just hang around waiting, I've got to get over there. Henk and the boys must have been notified by now. I quickly called Sam to let him know I was on my way.

I stopped on my way out the door, looking back at her. "Two tragedies in one week? What's happening?"

By the time I got to the Hendriks' farm, it looked like a macabre circus, with flashing red-and-blue lights and vehicles of every shape and size littering the area. Neighbours stood in tight groups, shock etched on their faces. Except for the occasional bright-orange flare, whipped up by the occasional gust of wind, the blaze was pretty much under control.

I pulled my car up close to the flapping yellow tape that read "Fireline Do Not Cross," that cordoned off the area around the barn. As I emerged from the car, the smoke and heat hit me like stepping into a furnace. While I stood there, heart racing, surveying the destruction, someone came up behind me and put their arm around my shoulders.

I looked up and under a yellow safety hard hat was the haggard, sooty face of my husband. "Have they found Edda yet?" I asked.

He bit down on his lip, shaking his head. "The explosion happened right around milking time." He squeezed me tighter.

Tears stung my eyes. "How... How could this have happened?"

"The neighbours heard a *boom* and called it in when they saw the flames. The fire chief thinks it was most likely caused by methane gas from the decomposing liquid manure. It's heavier than air, so the gas accumulates on the surface of the manure pool. It's noticeable by its rotten egg odor. We'll know more after the investigation, but it's been the cause of many animal and human deaths on farms."

We watched the firefighters dousing the errant flames, a veil of smoke surrounding the barn. "Barn fires are the worse," Sam said, "because of all the highly combustible items inside—wood, hay, fuel. It takes only minutes for them to get out of control."

I felt numb. "What about the cows?"

"Most are gone. Many died in the explosion, others from smoke inhalation. I read once that cows don't seem to fear fire like horses do. Strange, but they won't leave the herd or the barn. Sometimes if they manage to escape, they get confused and will run right back inside."

His eyes, red and watery from the smoke, softened as he pulled me closer. "Honey—if she wasn't in the barn she'd be standing here beside us right now. You need to prepare yourself for the worst."

My stomach sank, my chin trembling. "What about Henk and the boys?"

"They're here now. They decided to come home early and were going to surprise Edda. They were about two hours away when this happened. Henk blames himself for taking his time getting home. I told him he's crazy to think that way. It could have been far worse if they had been home sooner. The entire family could've been wiped out."

"So, you saw Henk?"

"Yes, he was running around here frantically. Such a sorry sight. Just imagine how he must have felt, with his wife probably trapped in the fire and his life's work going up in smoke. The horror of it all took its toll. The poor guy collapsed, and the paramedics had to carry him back up to the house. They're with him now. The boys are there, and Reverend Jim is there too." He looked around. "Police Chief Boyd is around here somewhere with the fire investigator. Why don't you go up to the house and stay with Henk until his sister and brother-in-law get here? Which should be in about an hour. I've got to get back." He gave me a quick kiss, then turned and took off running toward the barn.

"Be careful!" I yelled after him, watching as he disappeared into the chaos before me.

Before turning and heading up to the house, I spotted an SPCA helper at the far end of the barn, crouched in the blackened rubble, holding out a handful of hay, trying to entice one of the few surviving cows to approach her. I burst into tears.

CHAPTER TWELVE

Brynn

(Thursday, June 14)

STILL REELING FROM WEDNESDAY night's tragedy, I had to push myself to get up and go to work. I needed to keep busy; otherwise, my mind would slide into that deep, dark place.

Sam called up the stairs to tell me he was leaving for work and the coffee was on. I sat up, swung my legs over the side of the bed, and stared into space. My sleep last night had been fitful—waking every couple of hours.

I was glad that Henk and the boys now had family staying with them; I didn't want to intrude, so I left them to grieve on their own.

On my way to the pantry, I made a slight detour out to the bluffs overlooking the bay to pick up a fresh supply of strawberries and rhubarb from Ridgeview Organic Farms. All my store's produce was organic from area farms, when in season, or from our own hydroponic garden out back. This diversion, along with the fresh air and sunlight, helped to lift my spirits somewhat.

Now, back at the store, waiting by the side entrance for the Nature's Own van to arrive with a delivery of fresh asparagus, broccoli, green beans, and onions, I watched the people milling around outside picking up groceries, running errands, window shopping, and talking to their neighbours. Their daily lives, and mine, the same... while the Hendricks' lives had changed forever. *Somehow, it just didn't seem right.*

The aroma of freshly baked pastries wafting out through the door made me turn and have a look inside. Lori-Anne was carrying a tray of lemon squares out to the display area.

"Well, that's it for the baking," she said, wiping her hands down the front of her apron.

I gave her the thumbs-up, then called out, "If you're finished with that, maybe after you clean up in the kitchen, you can check on the hydroponics? Let me know if that overhead grow light is still flickering.

She nodded, undoing her apron and headed back into the kitchen.

Having a hydroponic garden was Sam's idea. He'd spent hours online researching the project, and after designing one specifically for our needs, he and Joe Chadwick built it. We were now able to produce our very own herbs, lettuce, spinach, kale, peppers and tomatoes.

My thoughts were interrupted by the tinkling of the front door bell. Georgie Fenwood walked in and waved to me.

"Hey Georgie," I waved back. "How are things at the B&B?"

"Good, just getting things ready for the long weekend ahead. We're fully booked. Lots to do." She made her way over to me and gave me a longer than usual hug. We separated; our eyes moist.

"I should be finished here in a few minutes," I said, looking at my watch. Then we can talk. Tea, coffee, and cold drinks are in the fridge down back. Feel free to help yourself."

"Thanks, don't mind if I do." She picked up a hand-carrier and headed down the aisle eyeing the produce. I saw her wander past the succulent display of strawberries in the window—then backed up, grabbed a basket and put it in her cart. After picking up a few more items, she made her way up to the cash register and put them on the counter. Popping a berry into her mouth, she smacked her lips together. "These are delicious, Brynn!"

"They're fresh from Ridgeview farm this morning," I called out.

The produce van finally arrived and off-loaded my order. Coming back inside, I picked up two warm lemon squares off the trolley, put them on a plate and headed down back to join her.

She was sitting at one of the two small mosaic-topped, wrought-iron tables sipping on a bottle of organic iced tea. I put the squares down on the table, made myself a coffee—third or fourth of the day—but who's counting? Then sat down beside her. "I still can't believe what happened."

She gave me a pained look. "We're all in shock."

I took a sip and put my mug down, staring into it. Finally, I looked back up. "I had this weird dream last night. I was a firefighter battling a blaze. I could see Edda through the dense smoke, but no matter how hard I tried getting to her, I couldn't make any progress. It was like I was running on a conveyor belt, but instead of going forward and getting closer to her, I was moving backwards and getting farther and farther away."

Puckering her lips after biting into the tangy, sweet-and-sour taste of the lemon tart, George nodded. "Hmm... Well, that's understandable after what has just happened."

I took a bite of my lemon square and licked the icing sugar off from around my mouth. "I have a book on dream interpretations; actually, it belonged to my gran. I keep it in my bedside table drawer. I pulled it out and checked the section on fires."

"So, other than the obvious—wishing you could have saved her, what other hidden meaning did it have?"

"Well, a fire can indicate a transformation or change, like the Phoenix rising out of the ashes after a fiery death, or spiritual awakening." I sipped at my coffee. "It can also mean a feeling of being overwhelmed or angry, and the smoke can foreshadow hidden or future trouble ahead." I hesitated; "I hate to mention it, but you know what they say—bad luck comes in threes."

"Geez!" she said, rolling her eyes. "I'm sorry I asked."

I took another bite of my lemon square and changed the subject. "Reverend Jim will be giving a eulogy at next Sunday's service—there won't be a dry eye in the place. A Celebration of Life has also been planned for the end of July. I'm sure most of the town will turn out. I hear the church and the Hendriks' neighbours have offered their help clearing away the rubble and organizing a barn-raising when Henk's ready. That's exactly what Edda would have wanted."

Georgie nodded.

The front door tinkled another arrival.

Excusing myself, I made my way to the front of the store. Even before I saw her, I knew who it was by the signature Chanel No. 5

perfume that drifted in through the door ahead of her. Lara Harding waltzed in, nose in the air, looking (as always) like she detected a foul odor in the air that nobody else could. However, in her defense, the nose job she had years ago *did* leave her with a permanent upturned, snotty look, which matched her attitude.

"Can I help you with anything Mrs. Harding?"

"Just thought I'd browse around. Anything you'd recommend today?"

"I've got fresh strawberries, gluten-free scones, and poppy seed loaves, and Lori-Anne just finished baking lemon squares. As always, I've got garden-fresh hydroponic veggies out back. Anything specific you're looking for?"

"Ah, no." Her gaze drifted around the shop, before settling back on me again.

I could feel her x-ray vision boring into me, a fake expression of concern painted on her face. "What a tragic accident at the Hendriks' farm." Leaning towards me, she lowered her voice. "Did you hear what caused the explosion? Does your husband know? I heard he's with the Emergency Task Force."

"The fire chief thinks methane gas was involved. That's all we know at this point. The fire department is still investigating."

Lara appeared to be listening intently, then . . . "Have you heard anything else about that hit-and-run in town? How's the police investigation going?"

I squinted at her, wondering why she was asking me about that.

"There is nothing new, as far as I know."

"I'm only asking because I heard it was you and your church friends that witnessed the accident."

"We didn't see much."

"What *did* you see?"

Why was she being so nosey? I was about to ask her as much when Georgie sauntered by looking at me, a smirk on her face. She wasn't a fan of Lara Harding, but then not many people in town were. "Hello, Mrs. Harding," she said stiffly.

"Oh, hello there," Lara said, startled. "I didn't know anyone else was in the shop."

Georgie forced a smile, then got busy searching for an item in the aisle nearby. I suspected she wanted to hear my conversation with Lara so she could discuss it with me later.

Lara turned back to me. "So, *did* you see anything?"

I sighed, "It's an on-going investigation so I really can't talk about it."

Lara stared at me for a long, uncomfortable moment before realizing no more news would be forthcoming, then glanced at her watch. "Oh, look at the time. I've got to go." She noticed the strawberries in the window and quickly hobbled over and grabbed a basket. Making her way up to the counter, she plunked a bill down, saying, "Keep the change," then limped towards the door.

"What's wrong with your leg?" Georgie called out.

"I twisted my ankle stepping off a curb. The doctor said it was just a sprain."

"Better put some ice on that."

"Yes, well, I did that. By the way, the hospital is having its annual Book-A-Thon the Saturday of the long weekend. Georgie, I know you belong to a book club and thought you might have some books you're willing to donate. I believe your friend Kaydee Wiebe is also a member. Would you mention the Book-A-Thon to her? I'll be around on the Friday before to pick the books up." With that, she turned and gimped out the door.

I came out from around the counter. "That was weird," I said, glancing at the door. "She never comes into my shop. She's up to something."

"Do you think she knows about you and Edda visiting Seymour at the meat plant?"

"I don't see how she could. I'm sure Seymour wouldn't have told her anything. He doesn't want anyone to know about the cheque, especially her. I just think she's being *nosey*, that's all."

CHAPTER THIRTEEN

Prissy

(Saturday, June 16)

PRISSY'S FREEDOM FROM SCHOOL or, the scholastic prison, as she liked to call it, was just a couple of weeks away. She could hardly wait. She hated taking orders. What good was school anyway? She wanted to be an actress—not a brain surgeon or mathematician.

She was a badass actress too, faking all those illnesses and never getting caught. Well, one time, forging her mom's signature on a note, she got busted when she spelled "orthodontist" wrong. Whoever invented that word must have had a lisp! Her mother said lying came as easily to Prissy as talking, and she certainly did more than her fair share of that.

She couldn't wait to get away from her mother and this crappy little town. Goodbye school, goodbye detention hall, and goodbye nosey neighbours. This would be the last summer she'd be stuck out here in the boonies, bored out of her skull, listening to her mother's whiny voice over and over. Her dad, the opposite of her mom, never said a word, which was even worse! When her mom nagged at him, he never stuck up for himself. He just took what she dished out. It was crazy! She wished just once he'd tell her off!

This afternoon was sunny and hot, great for hanging around the backyard pool and working on her tan. She thought about Dylan's little brother. That sucked big time. She told herself Dylan would eventually come around—he couldn't stay sad forever. Maybe now that nobody special was keeping him at home, he'd want to get his sorry ass out of town too.

Trying to get comfortable, she squirmed around in the lounger, and grabbing the hem of her crotch-cutting jean short-shorts, yanked them down. Her tube top, riding in the opposite direction, she pulled up. Finally getting settled, she opened her laptop and was about to check out bus fares to California when a mosquito landed on her arm. As she flicked it away, her computer slid off her lap and landed on the ground.

"Bloody Hell!" she shouted, and bending over, her ass-cheeks made an appearance. After picking up the computer and resting it back on her lap, she made herself comfortable again.

She began examining the bus schedules and fares in earnest now. She had big plans. Her mother was always giving her money, probably out of guilt for being such a crappy mother she thought. Prissy stashed the money away in an empty Kotex box in her bedroom closet. She planned to use the money for her and Dylan's big escape. A one-way ticket from Toronto to California by Greyhound was cheap with a company called Wanderu. It only cost $178. They'd take the Beckford bus to Toronto and then, after transferring to the Greyhound, they'd make their way down through the States. In two days, they would be in sunny L.A., where all the rich and famous movie stars lived. So what if the bus stopped in every hidey-hole town along the way? Laughing to herself, she realized the Wanderu slogan—*Free to Wanderu the Country*—clearly lived up to its name.

They'd go straight to her Aunt Mina's place and stay for as long as necessary. Prissy was only five when her aunt visited them in Canada—the one and only time. She didn't really remember Mina, but she knew a little about her from the stories her father told. Mina was his half-sister, and at least ten years older than him. She emigrated from the U.K. to the States in the sixties and settled in New York. When Mina was nineteen, and quite the looker, she'd married a rich, old Jewish guy with connections in the film industry. They'd moved to California, where he'd gotten her a bit part in a movie called *Beach Zombies*. Prissy found a copy of the 1960s film on Amazon and she and her friend, Tara, watched it. They almost peed themselves, laughing so hard.

In the movie, Mina played a gum-chewing receptionist. A zombie walks into the office with half his skull missing. His clothing, hanging in shreds, blood-stained, and tattered—his teeth chomping away with saliva drooling in ribbons down his chin. He mumbles something. Busy blowing a bubble while filing her nails, she doesn't bother to look up. The bubble keeps getting bigger and bigger until it's almost the size of her head—it finally pops. Then, slurping the sticky gum back in from around her lips, she continues chewing. Still not looking up, she says, "Go on in, Sir—Mr. Schumer is dying to see you."

That was it! One line of dialogue! Prissy couldn't help wondering how many takes was needed before Mina managed to blow a bubble that huge! According to Prissy's dad, Aunt Mina still gets a small residual whenever that movie is played, which would be about once in a blue moon. Mina's husband died years ago, leaving her with a pile of money. She now lives in a mansion in Los Feliz with her new partner, Leona.

Prissy guessed that living for years with a guy old enough to be her grandfather had probably turned her off men forever!

Prissy decided that she and Dylan would just show up at her aunt's house without warning. That way, it would be a lot harder for the old broad to turn them away.

She had it all figured out. While waiting for auditions, she'd work as a cocktail waitress at one of those fancy clubs, where if you flirted or flashed your boobies, you'd make more money in tips in a night than you would in a week. Meanwhile, Dylan could get a job as a car jockey. He loved cars, all kinds. She'd seen young couples like them hundreds of times in the movies.

Excited, she could hardly wait to call Dylan with her big plans. If she booked the bus tickets online now, they'd be ready to go right after graduation. A quote she'd read in a self-help book had stuck in her head: *The only person you are destined to become is the person you decide to be.* Well, she'd decided to be an actress, and nothing was going to stand in her way.

After closing her laptop, she couldn't help admiring the new charm bracelet dangling from her wrist. She twirled it around. It had pink beads with chains in between, and a silver skull with a cross dangling down. She remembered the rush she felt walking out of the Rainbow Magic store with this beauty in her pocket. She had developed a habit of *finger dipping*. Knowing she might get caught brought a sense of excitement to her life she felt was missing. Her mom eventually caught on to her pilfering habit and had taken her to see a doctor. He diagnosed Prissy with having OCD—caused by stress. She chuckled to herself thinking, not my fault—hers!

She got up, pulling down the hem of her shorts again, and walked over to the patio table to get her cell phone. Not seeing it there, she looked under the table, then went back and checked under the lounge chair cushion. Still nothing. She could have sworn she had brought her cell out with her. She was always misplacing that damned thing...
"*WTF?*"

Squiggling her feet into her flip-flops, she made her way through the patio doors into the house. "Ma! She yelled. Have you seen my frigging phone?"

"How would I know where you put the damn thing?" Lara yelled back, slipping her daughter's phone into her pocket.

CHAPTER FOURTEEN

Dylan

(Saturday, June 16)

DYLAN WAS IN HIS room, propped up on his bed, listening to iTunes when a text message came through on his phone. Seeing it was from Prissy, he quickly sat up on the edge of his bed and yanked the earphones out. His eyes narrowed with confusion as he stared in disbelief at the message.

Think it's time we called it quits. Stay cool. Priss.

What the hell was this? Her idea of a joke? Well, it wasn't funny. He shook his head smirking, then texted back...

Not funny Priss—stop kidding around. Let's take off to California right away. Ma and the kids will be fine. They've got the church women to help them. They don't need me around. What do u say?

Grinning, he waited for a reply, his foot drumming against the floorboards. Finally, his phone pinged.

I'm not kidding. I really mean it; I've met someone else. Too bad things didn't work out. Have a great life, just not with me.

He stared, dumb-founded—this didn't make any sense. They were in love! They had plans! They were going to L.A. together. She was the only thing that kept him going through all this turmoil and suffering. He stood up, pacing the room. His eyes wandered down to the message again, his grip tightening around the phone. It felt like a grenade he was holding; if this was true, with the pin already pulled—he felt dead inside.

It had taken him all last year working three nights a week after school at the mushroom farm to be able to afford this phone. He had become addicted to it, like an alcoholic or druggy to their fix. He even slept with it under his pillow, volume turned to max and vibrate. If he wasn't calling, texting, or Snapchating, he was doing what he did most of the time, even at school—playing Fortnite Battle Royale. He knew he was becoming more distant from his family and friends, but who cared?

He remembered his mother once asking him what he was doing all the time on his phone. He told her he was playing a game. She surprised him when she actually asked him about it.

"It's like the movie The Hunger Games. You've seen that movie on TV right?"

She nodded.

"Well, it's like that." His face lit up as he described it to her. "It's set in a futuristic earth where the players scavenge for weapons, armor, and resources and fight each other to the death in order to be the last player or team standing. You can play by yourself or in teams or just watch. Thousands of gamers are online at any one time playing. It's really—dope."

His ma had listened intently, then—"I think you spend way too much time on that phone. Time you got a real life. Do something useful for God's sake—anything!" Shaking her head, she turned and walked away.

He should have known she wouldn't approve. Why did he even think she would? No one ever did, except Priss. His mother was probably right, it *was* his escape from reality. His reality—sucked!

He looked at the text again, shaking his head. Just too weird! What he wanted to do was rush right over to her house and talk to her, but he knew he couldn't. He never understood why her mother, like, totally hated him. She would probably shoot him on sight. Not that he'd care, if Priss really meant what she said. But, of course, she couldn't have. Must be some kind of a sick game she was playing. He'd straighten this whole thing out when he saw her at school on Monday.

Meanwhile, he stuck his earphones back in his ears and turned up the iTunes volume. The song that was playing was by his favorite goth band Slipknot.

The Devil In I
'Undo these chains, my friend
I'll show you the rage I've hidden
Perish the Sacrament
Swallow, but nothing's forgiven
You and I can't decide which of us was taken for granted
Make amends, some of us are destined to be outlived
Step inside, see the Devil in I

Too many times, we've let it come to this
Step inside, see the Devil in I
You'll realize I'm not your Devil
I'm not your Devil anymore'

As the lyrics spoke to him, he sank deeper and deeper into despair.

CHAPTER FIFTEEN

Kaydee

(Sunday, June 17)

KAYDEE LOOKED FORWARD TO the end of the school year almost as much as her students. It gave her a chance to recharge her batteries and prepare for next year's curriculum. And the thought of not having to wake up to the annoying sound of the alarm clock would be a welcomed change. However, this past week she didn't have to rely on any alarm clock—she just couldn't sleep period. Ever since she and the church women made the big decision not to tell the police about the car logo, she hadn't slept a wink.

The large, glowing, orange numbers on the clock sitting on her nightstand read 4:30 a.m. It was Sunday morning, no need to get up early. And yet, here she was—wide awake. She still couldn't get over how quickly the other women had decided to keep the money. Yes, it would save the church and help out the Chadwick family, but Seymour ran a child down and left him there on the side of the road.

And now Edda was dead—God was punishing them!

SILENCE IS ~~GOLDEN~~ DEADLY

In fuzzy pink slippers and a long, flannel nightgown covered with pictures of little yawning owls, she made her way into the kitchen and went about making herself a mug of hot cocoa. Too impatient to wait before drinking the hot beverage, she quickly pulled her lips away, waving her hand in front of her mouth. Then, setting the mug down on the table to cool, she figured she might as well start her morning ritual of pulling the chains up on her cuckoo clocks. She had six of them. The hand-carved walnut clock with the ivy vines on the bottom, a stag's head on the top, a hare on one side, and a falcon on the other was her favourite. She bought it at a shop in Germany while travelling in Europe with her boyfriend, Harold. She remembered how much trouble they had getting it home. It was so large, it had to be shipped by sea and took two months to arrive. But it was worth the wait, and the money, as she listened to it playing *The Happy Wanderer*—alternating each hour between that and *Edelweiss*.

She loved her clocks, her companions—they kept her company. Since she had numerous allergies, she couldn't have pets or plants, so instead she collected cuckoo clocks. The clocks were set to go off a minute apart, this way each cuckoo could pop out and perform, instead of them all going off in one unrecognizable melee.

With her cocoa now in hand and James Patterson's novel *Deadly Secrets* tucked under her arm, she ambled into the living room and made herself comfortable in the big, beige overstuffed (somewhat like herself) chair. It made her feel safe and secure, like re-entering the womb.

The phone ringing jarred her awake, knocking the book off her lap. She grabbed the phone from the end table. "Hello?" she answered, glancing at the nearest clock, realizing she'd been asleep for hours. It was now 7:30 a.m.

"I'm sorry to bother you at home so early." It was a woman's voice. "I'm Kym Oldenberg's mother. My daughter is in your twelfth-grade homeroom class. I'm worried about her grades." She cleared her throat. "I know it's late in the year to be worrying about it now, with exams just around the corner, but she needs better grades for the Sheridan College scholarship. We certainly can't afford the tuition fees and, I was wondering if there's anything we can do—extra homework, tutoring, even summer school? We'll do whatever is needed." There was a pause. "I was hoping to meet with you in person to discuss it. Unfortunately, I just got out of hospital after having a hip replacement and can't get around. I was hoping you might be able to come out here—today if possible?"

Kaydee knew Kym as a good student, who, if she had only applied herself a little more would have done much better. She hated to see the girl miss out on a scholarship. Kaydee's students were her kids, and in a small town like Hubbs Harbour, one made the extra effort to help out. So, she reluctantly agreed.

It was a forty-five-minute drive from Hubbs Harbour down to Slough Bay where the Oldenbergs lived. The county being mostly rural farm country, kids were bussed to school from all over. Today, the sun beat down on her bright red 2005 Pontiac Sunfire, making the inside of the car live up to its name. The weatherman had called for hotter-than-average temperatures for the next few days. She looked over at the address scribbled on a scrap of paper lying on the passenger seat—1267 Pleasant Valley Road. The sign posted at the foot of the driveway just ahead was 1200. She was almost there.

The drive had been peaceful and the patchwork quilt of colourful farmland awe-inspiring but, she was feeling the heat. Her car air conditioner was broken again. The weather up till now had been great, and this was the first heat wave of the year. She grimaced remembering the weatherman's prediction of a higher-than-average pollen count over the next few days. The heat was suffocating. She rolled down the window to get some fresh air.

It wasn't long before her hay fever kicked in. Strange, but her allergen pills weren't in the medicine cabinet where they should have been. And, in her haste to leave the house, she didn't take any—this of all days! She grabbed a handful of tissues from the Kleenex box on the console between the front seats and dabbed at her eyes, then blew her nose. "Damn allergies," she muttered, tossing the used tissue into the garbage bag on the floor. She just missed the 1267 road marker and slammed on the brakes. Lucky for her, there was no car behind her. She backed up, then turned down the long rutted and dusty road leading to a house hidden behind a wall of evergreen trees. The big red-brick, Queen-Anne style house was in disrepair. The wraparound porch looked like it was sagging. The white paint was peeling off the wood trim and decorative gingerbread around the gables.

Kaydee knew there was a lot of new wealth in the county, especially now with city folks selling their expensive homes and moving out to the country, but there was still a lot of poverty here too—just hidden away, like old folks tucked away in nursing homes—out of sight, out of mind.

Getting out of the car, Kaydee had a sudden sneeze attack and grabbed a handful of tissues out of her purse, mumbling, "God, I hope I'm not going to be sneezing all day, or I won't get much done."

The floorboards of the front porch creaked as she cautiously made her way along to the front door. After a few steps, she froze, her eyes riveted on the big, fluffy, white cat sitting in the window watching her. Clutching her heart, she stepped back, ready to flee. Then, realizing the cat was on the inside of the house—not outside, she hesitated, telling herself it would be a waste of time coming all this way just to turn back now. She should at least ring the bell and let Kym's family know she's here.

With her eyes glued on the cat, she continued to the front door and pushed the buzzer. No response. Considering the condition of the house, she assumed the buzzer was probably not working, but she tried again anyway. There was still no answer, so she gave a good rap on the door. As the door creaked open, she jumped back. Then stepping closer, she called between the gap, "Hello, is anybody there?"

No answer.

She tried again, only louder this time. "Hello!"

A far-off voice called back, "Come in. I'm up-stairs. Come on up."

"No thanks," Kaydee answered. "I'll wait outside."

"I could really use help up here. *Please*!" Came the voice.

Kaydee's face twisted in debate; how could she resist a cry for help? Sticking her head inside the door and not seeing the cat anywhere around, she cautiously stepped into the house. Slowly she made her way across the foyer, looking both ways, like she was watching for cars—but instead, she was watching for cats. No sign of the cat anywhere. At the foot of the stairs, she scratched at her itchy hands as little red bumps appeared. *Oh shit*, she thought, *hives*. She called out again, "Mrs. Oldenberg, where are you?"

SILENCE IS ~~GOLDEN~~ DEADLY

"I'm up here, dear," came the response.

Kaydee continued up the stairs, her breathing laboured, her armpits wet. Resting on the landing partway up, she rummaged inside her bag, catching a whiff of a pungent odor. To her dismay, she realized that her deodorant wasn't able to keep up with the heat and the stress. Finally, her fingers grasped the inhaler. Taking it out of her bag, she gave it a shake, put it to her mouth, and pressed the pump. Nothing! Shaking it, she tried again—it was empty.

She stuck her hand back in her bag and this time, felt around for her EpiPen. When she couldn't find it, panic set in. She dumped the contents out on the landing, bent down and sifted through everything. The EpiPen wasn't there! Strange. Maybe it had fallen out in the car? With her heart racing, and her throat dry as desert dust, she put everything back in her bag, stood up, and decided to leave. Except for the sound of a clock ticking somewhere in the house, all was silent.

As she turned to go down the stairs—she stopped dead in her tracks. The big white cat she had seen earlier in the window was on his way up, along with a couple of his friends. She quickly spun around and started back up. She stumbled along the hall trying to keep ahead of the cats, her breath coming in short gasps. She managed to wheeze out, "Mrs. Oldenberg, what room are you in? I'm allergic to cats. Please help me."

With the cats in the hall inching ever closer, she heard a voice at the end of the hall. "I'm in here, dear."

Kaydee finally reached the room, and opening the door, leaned in. The room was dark; she couldn't see a thing. "Hello?" she said.

Suddenly, she was shoved from behind with such force she went flying ass over tea kettle into the room, landing splayed out on the floor. The door slammed shut behind her. When her eyes finally adjusted to the dark room, she beheld her worst nightmare . . . cats everywhere. They were sitting on the windowsill: curled up on the daybed, the vanity, and the dresser, and milling around on the floor. The stench from their feces and urine assaulted her nostrils. There was every shape and size of cat imaginable. With adrenaline pumping through her veins, she turned and managed to push herself up, staggering to her feet. She felt her throat and tongue swelling. She kept her eyes riveted on the cats as she backed up feeling for the door. When her backside finally hit the doorframe, she turned around, hands groping frantically for the doorknob. Finally finding it, she pulled . . .

The doorknob came off in her hand!

She stared at it, dumbfounded, like it was some kind of alien thing she'd never seen before. Try as she might, she couldn't get the doorknob back on, or get the door to open. She pounded on the door and tried calling out, but the only sound that came out of her mouth was a wheezy whisper. Exhausted, she turned and leaned against the door. Her knees buckled, and she slowly slid down—collapsing in a heap on the floor.

She felt like a bag of cement, unable to move. Her eyelids fluttered shut, but not before staring straight into the big, yellow eyes of the white feline perched contentedly on her stomach, purring away.

CHAPTER SIXTEEN

Brynn

(Wednesday, June 20)

AS SAM AND I made our way up the steps of the Field's Funeral Parlour, we noticed a young man standing off by himself near the front door. He was fidgeting with his tie, one leg shaking steadily like a kid loaded up on sugar. As we got closer, he looked at us through watery-blue eyes behind large, black-framed glasses and nodded.

"Hello. I'm Harold Meisner," he said stretching his hand out and limply shaking mine, then Sam's. "Thank you for coming. I am—I mean, I was, Kaydee's boyfriend."

I introduced myself as Kaydee's friend from church, and my husband. "We had hoped to meet you under better circumstances. We're so sorry for your loss."

He nodded again, then stuffing his hands into his trouser pockets, he stared down at the ground, obviously, out of his comfort zone. When he looked back up, I smiled at him and gave his arm a comforting rub. "It was nice meeting you, Harold. We'll see you inside," I said, heading in.

I whispered in Sam's ear, "Wow! So that's Kaydee's phantom boyfriend. All her friends had wondered about his existence. Although she'd talked about him often enough, nobody actually ever saw him—not at church, her home, or in any of the shops or restaurants around town. We were wondering if he really existed."

It looked like it was going to rain at any moment as dark clouds passed overhead, and rumbling claps of thunder echoed through the sky. It reminded me of what my grandma, Mumsie, said to me after my father's death when I was a little girl. She said when you hear thunder at a funeral, it means the spirit of the dearly departed has made its way up to heaven. As we entered the lobby, mourners were standing around in pairs and small groups talking, some dabbing at their eyes.

I saw Sophie come in through the front door and waved to her. When she finally made it over to us, she gave us both a big hug.

"Did you see Kaydee's boyfriend, Harold, at the door?" I asked.

"Yes," she said. "So, he's nae a phantom after all. Poor laddie looks a mess. He's going to miss her. Guess he's standing in for her family. Her parents live down in Florida—her mother has Alzheimer's, and her father's health nae good either. And, she has few relatives that I know of."

Just then, I heard giggling. I glanced around and saw some of Kaydee's students huddled together in a far corner of the room hidden behind the oversized floral arrangement sitting on a round pedestal table—a tribute from the school. Prissy Harding and a small group of her peers, clearly seemed more interested in themselves than the dearly departed. Steps away, Trish, her partner Liz, and Georgie and her husband Hugh were talking to Police Chief Boyd. Trish caught my eye and motioned us over.

"Chief Boyd was just telling us about his trip out to the Oldenburgs' place," Georgie said. All eyes shifted towards the Chief.

"The Oldenbergs' neighbour, Mildred Pierce, found the body," he said. "She was minding the place while they were away in Barrie for a few days visiting Ethel's sick mother. She had noticed a car parked up by the house, and got curious when it was still there in the evening when she went back to feed the cats. She was surprised when she didn't see any of the strays milling around outside waiting to be fed. She then went inside to feed the house cats and do a check through the house. That's when she found Kaydee. It appears Kaydee got herself trapped in an upstairs room. She must have panicked when she couldn't get out. When the neighbour finally got the door open, she said the room was full of cats. The coroner's report said she died from anaphylactic shock. Looks like her allergies and asthma basically suffocated her. Her tongue swelled so much it blocked her air passage; she couldn't breathe and suffocated!"

"How terrible! Does anyone know why she was out there?" I asked.

"She had a briefcase full of Kym's schoolwork, tests, assignment marks, and the like. Looks like she might have been going out there to discuss Kym's grades. The thing is—the Oldenbergs weren't even home. We're in the process of checking phone records to see if that can shed any light on why she was there. Her neighbour said the Oldenbergs' had about six house cats but fed a large number of strays that roamed the area. She also said the Oldenbergs' had a habit of leaving their door unlocked. They felt safe and didn't worry about the place being robbed. They figured there was nothing to rob. The big question is how did all the cats, including the strays, end up in that one room? It's a strange one all right!" he said, shifting his weight from one foot to the other and scratching his jaw.

"Kaydee must have been terrified," Trish said, her eyes filling with tears.

Charlie continued. "The set screw connecting the doorknob to the square shaft that operates the old-fashioned door latch had come loose and must have come off in her hand when she pulled on it. Looks like she tried desperately to get out, but the door wouldn't open. There were bruises on her hands, along with several broken, bloodied fingernails. Her inhaler was later found on the stair landing. Empty!"

I gasped, my heart aching for Kaydee.

Near the end of the service, we made our way out of the funeral home, brushing past Seymour and Lara Harding, who were chatting up a couple I didn't know.

Outside, the clouds had passed, and the sun was out. It felt good to be out in the warm light of day. I noticed Dylan standing out front under a clump of birch trees, hands in his pockets, watching as people exited the church obviously waiting for someone to come out.

Prissy Harding came out the door ahead of her parents and, seeing Dylan, made a beeline straight for him. Seymour and Lara following along behind her, passed by us without saying a word. Seymour ignored us, but I could feel Lara's eyes linger on me. Finally, looking away, she noticed her daughter heading toward Dylan. Lara hot-footed after her. A few eyebrows raised as she yanked her daughter's arm and dragged her away. With Prissy squirming in her mother's grasp, they headed for the parking lot. I heard Lara hiss to her daughter as they passed by us, "You stay away from that boy or *else*!"

CHAPTER SEVENTEEN

JOE

(Wednesday, June 20)

JOE CHADWICK SLUMPED ON a barstool at the local legion, nursing yet another beer—his liquid sustenance these days. His taste for food was gone, along with his interest in almost everything. Emmett, the bartender, gave him *the look* as he picked up the empty glass and took it over to the sink. Joe recognized that *look*, he'd seen it many times before—pity. He had become the town's hard luck case. He hated being unable to give his family the life they deserved, and now, the unthinkable happened . . . his son Trevor was dead! He felt like he was sinking down into a black hole, with all he ever cared about being sucked in along with him. And now with the plant closing, he'd never make ends meet with only his measly veterans disability pension to reply on.

He slid off the barstool and hobbled down the hall to the washroom to take a piss. Looking in the mirror, he didn't recognize the thin, haggard face with the dark stubble staring back at him. He rubbed at his bloodshot eyes and snickered, remembering how the high school girls used to say he looked like Tom Cruise. The only thing they had in common now was their five-foot-seven-inch frame. His shorter legs, certainly hadn't affected his running ability. He was the star runner on the track-and-field team, then he switched to football. Football was king with the girls, and he became the best running back in the school league that year.

He returned from the bathroom, slid back onto his stool at the bar and motioned for Emmett to bring him another beer.

Emmett brought one over and, putting it down on the counter, eyed Joe. "Hey Joe, how about a sandwich—on the house! What can I get for you . . . ham and cheese, salami? Hey, I know," he said raising an eyebrow. "How about a corned beef on rye?"

"No thanks, Emmett. Not hungry," Joe lifted his glass and took another swig.

Emmett shook his head. "You really should eat something," he said, turning and going back into the kitchen.

Joe used to enjoy swapping war stories and having a few brewskies with his fellow vets, but not anymore. Now, he just sat there wallowing in self-pity. Still, the Legion was his home away from home, and about the only thing he didn't do here at his favourite watering hole was sleep. Every night after he'd had enough beer to pickle an elephant, he'd curl up in the back seat of his car and sleep it off till the sun came up. If the weather got too hot, he'd claim a bench in the park. Late evenings in the park were peaceful under the big red maple at the far end, and nobody bothered him there.

His mind flashed back again to Seymour Harding. He'd love to knock that SOB off his pedestal. They had been best buddies in high school, until Seymour stole Betty. Then, after knocking her up, he dumped her like a bag of trash and turned his sights on the more lucrative Lara Gavin (now Lara Harding). Lara didn't have the looks or personality of Betty, but her father made millions from an environmentally clean, *supposedly* safe fracking technique he invented that extracted oil, gas, and geothermal energy from the earth's bedrock.

Meanwhile, Betty had left town to escape all the gossip and stayed with her aunt in Toronto. Unfortunately, she left before graduating high school. Two years later she returned to the county with a little boy in tow.

Emmett brought out a plate with a corned beef on rye and a dill pickle and put it down in front of Joe. "Eat this," he ordered.

Joe took a bite out of the pickle, then pushed the plate aside. He took another slug of beer, his thoughts returning now, as they always eventually did, to Kandahar.

After graduating high school, he joined the army. A year later he was deployed to the Nathan Smith Base in Kandahar, Afghanistan—along with a thousand Canadian troops—as part of the Medusa Offensive. While out on regular patrol in the dessert, his jeep hit a landmine. He remembers coming to, lying in the sand, his eyes focusing on a single, dusty boot a few yards away with a bloody stump sticking out of it. He hadn't realized until he saw the ragged, bloody end of his own leg that the boot was his. After weeks spent rehabilitating at the Landstuhl Medical Centre in Germany, he returned home. He was lucky—many of his buddies returned home in a box. By then, Betty was back in the county. They were reunited and married a year later. Seymour gave him a job at his meat-packing plant, which Joe felt was purely out of guilt and pity. *After all, Joe was raising Seymour and Betty's son, Dylan, as his own.*

Now that asshole was closing the meat-packing plant, putting lots of good people out of a job. And why? Because the employees had mustered up enough guts to form a union—that's why.

"I'm just going out for a smoke," he called to Emmett who was in the kitchen. He gulped down the rest of his beer, slid off the seat, and hobbled outside. He lit his cigarillo, and taking a long drag, he thought about the latest horrific events.

While at the Grant's house trimming bushes under the open window, he thought he heard something about Seymour's car hitting his boy. Then the window had thumped shut. He stopped in mid clip, his mind racing; heat rising to his face. He was ready to go right over to the Hardings and strangle that bastard. But had he heard what he thought he heard? Maybe he was wrong. Why else hadn't the women gone to the police with this information? He really hated the church, and those do-gooder church women. *Where was God in Kandahar, eh? Where was God when Deedee was born disfigured? Where was God when Trevor was killed? Where, oh bloody where?*

Then, he started thinking back to that fateful Friday night. He had arrived home earlier than usual totally shit-faced, and left again soon after to go back to the Legion. He stumbled around back of the house to take a piss, and was stunned to see Seymour's black sedan parked there. He'd never been more surprised. He knew Seymour would never be caught dead slumming around this neighbourhood. He looked inside the car. It was empty, but he saw the keys dangling from the visor. Then it dawned on him—the Harding brat was probably upstairs with Dylan.

He'd seen the way they looked at each other. There was a connection between them all right, but it was more than puppy love!

He started gimping back to the house to confront them, then changed his mind. It was the Big Man he wanted to confront, tell him exactly what he thought of him—tell him to his face what a steaming piece of shit he was.

His old Ford pick-up truck sat back there by the trash bins, a metal boot clamped on the back wheel, put there after his last DUI charge. He remembered getting into Seymour's car and driving into town in the dense fog, and he vaguely remembers hearing a *thump* and thinking he'd hit a garbage can. Since he had been driving without a license, and drunk, he knew he couldn't stop, so he'd stepped on the gas and took off. Finally, he had enough sense to realize the trouble he could get into if caught, so he drove the car back to the house and left it where he found it. He figured he'd get around to confronting Seymour another day; what he needed now was another drink. He was not sure how, but he managed to make his way back to the Legion. Maybe a car had stopped and picked him up taking pity on a cripple, or maybe he made it into town under his own steam—it was only a few blocks away and he'd done it before. He couldn't remember. The next morning, he'd found himself waking up on the park bench.

When he heard the news about Trevor being killed in a hit-and-run accident, he felt as if he'd been sucker-punched. Was it possible... had he killed his own son?

CHAPTER EIGHTEEN

Brynn

(Wednesday, June 20)

IT WAS LATE AFTERNOON as I made my way along the stone path, past the ornate plaque hanging from a black, wrought-iron staff out front. It proclaimed "The Historic Fenwood House, B&B, Circa 1880."

The red brick century house, built by prosperous United Empire Loyalists, had been through many reincarnations, with the latest being this up-scale bed-and-breakfast. Brynn knew Georgie and Hugh always admired this house. So, when Hugh retired from the air force ten years ago and the house came up for sale, they bought it and converted it into its present form. The extra cash from the business went toward their vacations abroad, as well as keeping them from getting bored.

Georgie saw me through the window and waved.

Once inside, after quick hugs at the door, I followed her down the hall. The high, ten-foot ceilings, original wide-plank pine flooring and fancy Victorian millwork always impressed me. We passed through the dining room with its huge, stone, wood-burning fireplace and into the lounge.

Sophie and Trish sat there sipping wine from the beautiful German crystal wine glasses Georgie brought back from Hugh's stint in Lahr, Germany.

Georgie offered me a glass, which I readily accepted. She returned a minute later carrying two glasses—one for herself and one for me.

The fact that there were only four, and not six of us present, seemed strange. I raised my glass, "A toast to our beloved friends, who will be sorely missed. May they rest in peace." We sat there in silent for a moment thinking of our friends and trying to absorb the dreadful events of the past two weeks.

Trish broke the silence. "You'll never guess who I saw at the mushroom farm last week." All eyes turned her way. "I usually don't work the afternoon shift but, last Monday I did. Around noon I was getting my lunch out of my locker to take back to the lunchroom, when who do I see looking into the locker room, but Lara Harding. She looked surprised to see me. I was stunned she even recognized me with my coveralls, hard hat, and hair net on. She said she just finished buying a pound of mushrooms at the plant's retail outlet and was waiting for Seymour. He was in the office visiting the plant manager, an old golfing buddy of his. Then—she gives me that look—you know the one." Trish does her impersonation of Lara by raising her chin and looking down her nose. The rest of us can't help but chuckle.

"And then she says to me, I didn't know you worked here. Why would she? She's never said more than two words to any of us. Stuck-up, bitch."

"Now Trish! We all know what the lassie's like, try and be more—Christian." Sophie winked at us. We all grinned, then fell silent again.

Georgie spoke up. "I don't understand what's happening—the Chadwick boy, Edda, and now Kaydee all dead. All accidents?" She got up to get the tray of cheese and crackers I saw sitting on the kitchen counter. "Seems pretty strange to me." She said, putting the tray down on the table in front of us.

Trish reached over; a small rainbow tattoo peeked out on her upper arm from under her short-sleeved black T-shirt. She cut off a hunk of Spanish Manchego cheese, and grabbed a cracker off the tray. "I just can't figure out how Kaydee ended up in a room filled with cats!"

"Aye, it all seems mighty suspicious," Sophie said, staring into her wine glass. Then, glancing back up, "Is it just me, or is anyone else thinking what I am—that these so-called accidents—weren't really accidents?"

I had just smeared Brie on my cracker. "So, what are we talking about here?" I said, looking around. "If not accidents, what? Murder? At least, someone has guts enough to say what I'm sure we've all been thinking. Strange how Kaydee's inhaler was empty; she didn't have her EpiPen, and she ended up in a room full of cats! Seems so unlikely.

"But who? Why?" Georgie said, tilting her head to one side, a puzzled look on her face.

"Seymour," I said, finally sliding the cracker into my mouth. "He's the only person I can think of with a motive to want us out of the picture. After all, we took his money. Maybe he's worried we'll still go to the police after all, or want more money."

Georgie frowned. "That's ridiculous. I can't believe he'd kill two people to cover up an accident. Horrible accidents do happen to people." She shook her head saying, "I think we've all been watching too many episodes of *Dateline* and *20/20* on TV."

Sophie looked at her. "Maybe, maybe not. I heard through the grapevine, that he's been having financial difficulties, what with building the new plant and all."

Trish stiffened in her chair. "Should we go to the police?"

"Aye . . . and tell them what?" said Sophie.

I could feel the colour draining from my face. "The truth," I said. "We don't want any more—*accidents*."

Georgie mumbled, "We might all be put in jail."

It was quiet again.

"What we need now that our main eyewitness, Edda, God bless her soul, is no longer with us, is evidence. Time to start digging around." I eyed Sophie. "I'm going to drive out to Slough Bay in the morning and have a look around. Would you like to come along?"

"To be sure, lassie, four eyes are better than two."

CHAPTER NINETEEN

Brynn

(Thursday, June 21)

ON OUR WAY THROUGH town the next morning, Sophie and I stopped at the police station, hoping Chief Boyd might have some new information he could share with us.

As we entered the station, I took off my sunglasses and stuck them on top of my head. It took a minute for my eyes to adjust. The inside of the station was dark compared to the unblemished bright sky outside. When my eyes adjusted, I could see Charlie through the reception window at the front counter picking up his messages.

As we walked up to the window, I called out. "Hi Charlie."

He looked up and came over. "Hi, ladies. What's up?"

"We were just wondering if there were any updates on the hit-and-run accident or Kaydee's death," I said.

He glanced at his watch and waved us in. "I've got a few minutes," he said.

We made our way down the hall passing by rooms on either side—Briefing Room, Squad Room, Sargent's Office, Interview Room, Admin, and so forth, until we came to the Police Chief's Office.

His office was small, with stacks of file folders littering the floor, windowsill, top of the filing cabinet, and his desk. He grabbed a pile of folders sitting on one of the chairs and set them on the floor, then brought the chair over to join the one already sitting in front of his desk. He motioned for us to take a seat.

"Sorry for the mess, but believe it or not, these are all cases I'm working on, and though it doesn't seem like a system, it's my system and I know where and what every file is."

"We understand, laddie," Sophie grinned as we sat down.

Charlie leaned back in his office chair, put his hands behind his head and his feet up on the corner of his desk—the only square inch of free space.

"There's nothing new to report on the hit-and-run. A couple of people witnessed a large, black car racing through town around the time of the accident, but they didn't get a plate number or make of the car. Not much help there—large, black cars are as abundant as dandelions in the spring. We're contacting garages and repair shops within a one-hundred-mile radius to see if a large black car was brought in for accident repairs."

My face reddened as I felt a pang of guilt knowing full well whose car it was, and I was sure Sophie felt the same.

Sophie asked, "What about Kaydee's investigation? Is there any anything new there?"

"Well, generally, I wouldn't talk about an ongoing investigation. But seeing as you ladies are the closest thing to a family she has—his feet came down from the desk and he leaned forward looking at us. "The phone records finally came in, and the call history on Kaydee's phone showed a call was placed from a cell phone at the Oldenberg residence that morning. The thing is—it wasn't Ethel Oldenberg. They weren't even home at the time. It sounded like a woman's voice asking Kaydee to come over and help Kym with her final exams."

Sophie and I glanced at each other, then quickly looked back at the chief, hanging on his every word.

"Mrs. Pierce, the neighbor who monitors the place when they're away, said she tried opening the upstairs door but found it blocked. She pushed on the door and finally got it partly opened. She was shocked to see an arm lying on the floor on the other side of the door and realized she had been pushing against a body. When she finally got the door open, a clutter of cats ran out. A woman was lying on the floor, so Mrs. Pierce quickly checked for a pulse, couldn't find one, and immediately dialed 911 on her cell. We arrived at the scene minutes after the ambulance arrived. It was too late for resuscitation. They pronounced Kaydee dead at the scene."

I shook my head. "How dreadful."

"Poor lassie," Sophie said, a swallow catching in her throat.

The chief continued, "The Oldenbergs have been very cooperative. Hopefully, we can get to the bottom of this." He stepped out from behind his desk, signaling the meeting was over, and walked us out to the lobby.

SILENCE IS ~~GOLDEN~~ DEADLY

∼

Sophie and I made our way down to Slough Bay in the southern part of the county. We drove past acres of bright yellow canola, lush green sugar beets, and eye-popping lavender and passed by a couple of "u-pick" strawberry farms with people out in the fields, bent over, picking (and eating) the berries.

A little further along, we saw a handwritten cardboard roadside sign announcing "Fresh Brown Eggs Ahead," and we turned down the next driveway. To our left was a miniature, red, barn-shaped chicken coop with an attached large, wire enclosure, where we saw Road Island Reds clucking about, scratching in the dirt, doing their chicken thing.

While most homes in the Slough Bay region of the county were old clapboard farmhouses, the Pierce's residence was a modern grey-brick bungalow. I heard the drone of a lawn mower long before seeing a man come scooting around the corner of the house perched on a riding mower. As I climbed out of the car, I caught a whiff of the newly mown grass. A few fluffy, white clouds drifted across the clear blue sky, topping off the serene setting.

A woman with short, curly, salt-and-pepper hair came out of the screened front door onto the stoop, smiling. "Hello there," she said. "Are you here to buy eggs?"

"Hello," I answered, "I'm Brynn and this is Sophie. We're from the Hubbs Harbour United Church, and we were hoping you might spare us a few minutes. The woman who had the accident over at the Oldenbergs' place, Kaydee Wiebe, was our friend.

"Yes, I've seen you ladies at the church from time to time," she said, coming down the steps and introducing herself as Mildred Pierce. "That poor soul. I'm so sorry about your friend."

After a pause, Mildred gazed up at the sky, hands on her hips. "It's such a beautiful day, why don't we take a seat in the gazebo around back. Just follow the flagstone path," she said, pointing. "I'll go inside and get us a cold drink."

We made ourselves comfortable in the back garden. Mildred returned about ten minutes later carrying an old, metal, Pepsi-Cola tray with plastic tumblers, and a plastic pitcher of icy lemonade. Lemon slices floating on top. She set it down on the table, then pulled up a chair. "So, how can I help you?" she asked, pouring our drinks.

"We're just trying to understand what happened," I said. "The police said she died in a room full of cats. We're wondering how all the cats got into that one room. She was allergic to cats. We can't figure out why she'd even go in there. We owe it to her to try and find out—it's so strange."

"Yes, strange indeed," Mildred said, shaking her head. "But I told the police everything I know. I can't add much. The feral cats never go inside. I always feed them outside; I haven't got a clue why, or how, they all got in there."

"Any ideas how they *might* have gotten in there?" Sophie asked.

"They must have been lured inside, is all I can figure. But they're very skittish, and why would anyone do that?" Mildred took a sip of lemonade. "Well, I suppose they could have been trapped outside and brought inside. It wouldn't be that hard; especially if you knew when and where they got fed. All you would need is a big enough cage, put it where they normally feed, and then rub good-smelling stuff on it, like sardine oil. Put some appetizing food inside; maybe tuna and cover the cage with camouflage. If they're hungry, they'll go in!"

"Who else knows when you feed the cats?" I asked.

"I really don't know. The Oldenbergs are usually home. It's just recently, with her mother ailing, that they've been going up to Orillia to check on her."

"Are you the only one who feeds the cats when they're away?" I took another sip.

"Yup, pretty much. My husband Earl and I are around most of the time. I don't mind, those feral cats are God's critters too. When we go away, they feed our chickens for us. You know, tit for tat."

Sophie chuckled. "Or in your case—chick for cat."

Both Mildred and I grinned, shaking our heads.

We finished our lemonade and thanked Mildred for her hospitality. Then after buying a few dozen eggs to take back to my store, we headed over to the Oldenbergs' place.

CHAPTER TWENTY

Brynn

(Thursday, June 21)

THE OLDENBERGS' HOUSE HAD seen better days. It surprised me, further highlighting the fact that poverty exists in the county. It wasn't all just rich, transplanted city folk. Most of the small farms dotting the countryside barely eked out enough to feed the farmer and his family. If you weren't employed by one of the big three companies or the municipality, the only jobs left were mainly in the service areas, mostly catering to the seasonal tourists and paying minimum wage. Working at the wineries fell into the latter category. Only the wealthy winery owners made money, and they had to have plenty of bucks to invest in the money-sucking business in the first place. Many of the smaller mom and pop operations barely squeaked by.

It's fortunate that foodbanks, grocery stores, churches, and emergency services organize food drives; otherwise, people wouldn't be aware of poverty.

Sophie and I made our way across the uneven floorboards to the front door. Several cats lying there sleeping in the sun woke up and took off.

Sophie knocked on the door. It was answered almost immediately by a woman in her late fifties, medium height, slight of build, with short-cropped brown hair. Her eyes were red-rimmed and looked like she either had an eye infection, or hadn't slept well for days. She wiped her hands off on a stained, flowered apron.

"Yes?" she said with a forced smile.

We introduced ourselves and said we were church friends of the woman who had the unfortunate accident here.

She eyed us suspiciously, looking from one to the other.

"We know you've already spoken with the police," I said, "but we were hoping you wouldn't mind answering a few questions for us?"

"What do you want to know?"

"We were wondering if you've seen anything unusual around here lately, or anyone hanging around?"

"We've just got back from being away for a few days, but no, I've noticed nothing unusual. It's quiet here and being well away from the road, we don't see much." She paused, then tapping her finger against her bottom lip said, "The Harding girl was over visiting with Kym last week, and Joe Chadwick was here a while back to take out branches and logs from downed trees in the woods out back for firewood, but nothing unusual."

I started to speak, but was interrupted.

"Please, call me Ethel," she said, looking more relaxed and softening her tone.

"Ethel, where do you normally feed the strays?" I asked.

"Around back. I put cat food in empty plastic margarine tubs and spread them around and under the stoop."

"What do you usually feed them?"

"Mostly dry cat food, some canned we get free from pet stores in the area when it's near or at expiry. Folks who know we look after the strays also donate food or money."

"You must have a lot of strays around?" Sophie said.

"We do. There are about fifteen or so now. That number keeps changing. New ones arrive and some of the regulars disappear. They die over the winter or get eaten by coyotes. Once or twice a year, Joe Chadwick comes over and catches any new ones and we take them to be spayed or neutered. Dr. Nadula at the Hillsdale Veterinary Clinic does it for free."

"Would you mind if we have a look around outside?" I asked.

"The police just finished searching the area, but sure, I don't mind. You go right ahead."

We thanked her and as Ethel closed the door, we headed down the porch steps and started looking around.

"What are we looking for, lassie?" Sophie rubbed her chin, her forehead wrinkling.

"I don't know, something, anything!"

"I'm sure the Barneys have combed the whole area thoroughly."

"Barneys?" My eyebrows raised.

"You know Bobbies, Coppers, Smokey-the-Bears!"

I couldn't help smiling. "Well, you never know. It doesn't hurt to have a look." I pulled a couple of little black plastic, biodegradable doggie poop bags from my pocket. "Here, take these," I said, handing a couple to Sophie. "Just in case you find anything, we don't want to contaminate it."

We slowly drifted apart, each looking around and kicking through the long grass. Heading around back, we saw a few empty, plastic margarine tubs strewn around, with bits of dried cat food stuck to the inside.

Sophie bent down and looked under the stoop. Suddenly, she sprang straight up in the air. "Michty me!" she yelled as a large black cat ran out from under the stoop, hissed, and took off. "That moggy just about scared me ta death," she said, holding her hand over her heart.

I cracked up laughing as the cat, more frightened of Sophie, sprinted off around the corner of the house. A mild breeze rustled the leaves as I shuffled along through the grass heading over to a small stand of poplar trees on the far side of the property. Something shiny caught my eye and I was just about to reach down and pick it up when I remembered to use a baggie. Opening the bag, I slipped it over my hand and picked the item up. It was only an empty crumpled cigarette pack, the inside foil reflecting the sun. I tied the bag shut and slipped it into my purse.

"Found something?" Sophie asked coming up alongside me.

"Just an empty cigarette pack. How about you?"

"Nae much," she said shaking her head. "Just this wee broken, black plastic box."

After searching for almost an hour, we decided we weren't going to find much else.

"Maybe we should ask to have a wee peak inside," said Sophie.

I agreed, and we headed back around to the front door. Ethel was already waiting at the door before we arrived, like she had been watching us through the window and was expecting a knock on the door any minute. A large white cat ran out the opened door.

We apologized for bothering her again and then I asked, "Ethel, we hate to impose, but would it be possible to have a quick look at the room where they found Kaydee?"

Ethel cast a skeptical eye at us, but after a slight hesitation, said, "I guess so," and stepped aside for us to enter.

We walked through the sparsely furnished living room. There was a large, brown couch covered in cat hair against one wall, with two of the culprits sleeping on it. A small, plain, pine oval coffee table in front of it. A dark green, lazy-boy chair also covered in cat hair sat in one corner, and a small T.V. on a stand occupied the opposite corner. The floor was old, pine, boarding that continued up the stairs, and I guessed it probably ran throughout the house.

Ethel led the way up the stairs and down the hall. As we walked along, the occasional floorboard creaked like an old person's complaining bones. A cat could usually be seen wandering about.

Ethel stopped in front of the last door on the right-hand side of the hall. "In there," she said pointing. "I haven't been in yet to clean it up. The police just finished yesterday."

"Ethel, if the doorknob came off in Kaydee's hand, you must have noticed it being loose for a while now?"

"No, can't say as I have. But then, I don't go into that room much. It's just for storage." She paused waiting for another question, then,

"I've got to get back downstairs. I'm doing up strawberry preserves. Just let yourselves out when you're finished." She turned and headed back down the hall toward the stairs.

I quickly called after her, "Ethel, does anyone in the house smoke?"

Ethel stopped and turned a questioning eye to me. "No," she said emphatically, we can't afford to have our money go up in smoke!" Frowning and shaking her head at such a stupid question, she continued along the hall and disappeared down the stairs.

The hallway was long, with three doors on each side. The middle room on the left was the bathroom. There was a small window at the end of the hall, partially open with grey sheers hanging on either side being tussled about by the slight breeze. I figured Ethel was trying to air the place out.

The door to the room we wanted to check was open, so we entered. It was warm, and airless, and it smelled. I tried the light switch. When the light didn't come on, I noticed the light fixture in the ceiling was missing its bulb. It was a small room, the ceiling gabled at one end with a small curtain-less dormer window. The room looked like it was being used for storage. It contained a few pieces of old furniture, including a futon, dresser, a couple of old wooden chairs and a number of stacked plastic bins.

We browsed around the room. I walked over to the dormer window, pushing aside a few cobwebs and tried opening it. It wouldn't budge. Upon further inspection, I noticed it was painted shut. Pulling a face, I realized what the stench was—cat feces and dark urine stains were all over the floor.

Sophie waved her hand in front of her face, trying to fan away the odour. "Phew—Moggie toilet!"

Before leaving the room, I checked out the door. The doorknob was back on. I opened and closed it a few times. The door stuck a bit, and I had to jiggle the handle each time to get it open. Not unusual, I thought, with the settling a house this age goes through. There was no lock on the door.

"Strange how that doorknob came off in her hand."

"Maybe the lassie was so terrified she had an extra boost of adrenaline strength. We've all heard of a mother being able to lift a car off a 'wee one' pinned under it, or a parent fighting off a bear to protect their young'uns."

I looked at her quizzically. "Maybe."

We headed back downstairs, and at the front door, I called back a thank you to Ethel.

"It still doesn't add up," I said, as we walked to the car. "Who called Kaydee to come over here, and why would all those cats be in that room? It really looks more and more like a setup. The screw in the door handle could have been loosened or taken out on purpose. But why Kaydee, and who?"

CHAPTER TWENTY-ONE

Trish

(Friday, June 22)

TRISH LEANED BACK IN the bright red Muskoka chair, draining the last drop of chardonnay from her glass. "That was a great dinner, Liz," she said to her partner, her hand patting her full belly. Contented, she gazed around their compact backyard admiring all that she and Liz had accomplished since moving into the cottage two years ago.

To supplement their income as artists, Trish worked at the mushroom farm. They planned to renovate the garage into an art studio, where they would give lessons in painting and jewelry making. The late-night shift at the mushroom farm from 7:00 to 2:00 a.m. worked out well, as it gave Trish the freedom to paint during the day. However, she felt like she was burning the candle from both ends. Luckily, they had almost reached their goal, so she wouldn't have to put up with this job much longer.

Liz made beautiful jewelry from beach glass, she collected on her frequent visits to the lakeside parks. However, Trish's forte was painting with wax. Encaustic painting, also known as hot wax painting, is one of the oldest surviving art forms, going back to the first century B.C. It involves adding coloured pigments to a heated wax medium usually applied on tile or wood. Building the wax up layer upon layer added texture and depth to the paintings. Trish found the process pleasantly cathartic. It was the closest one can get to sculpting on a two-dimensional surface.

She imagined how long and involved it must have taken the artists centuries ago. But now, with the advent of heat guns, heat lamps, hairdryers, and hotplates, and with wax being available in many forms at hobby stores, this art form was making a comeback. She was eager to start teaching this updated ancient art form to a new generation.

Their step-saver backyard was a well-manicured circle of lawn surrounding a flag-stoned patio the couple put down when they first moved in—keeping lawn mowing to a minimum. A white, wooden picnic table with life-like ladybugs and bees painted on it by Liz sat in the middle. Scattered round the patio were planters filled with geraniums and cascading ivy. And with the help of their church friends, they planted perennial beds around the lawn edges. Their tulips and daffodils had graced the tables at many church functions. Their barbecue was conveniently located just outside the patio doors leading into the kitchen.

Trish picked one of the few remaining tulips, remembering how Kaydee and Edda, along with their other church friends, had spent countless hours in the backyard eating, drinking, and laughing while planting bags of bulbs.

Glancing down at her watch, she was surprised at the time. "Geez, Liz. It's six-thirty already. I've got to get going or I'll be late."

Liz, contentedly sitting in one of the Muskoka chairs, waved a hand toward the dishes on the picnic table. "Don't worry about this mess; just get going! Are you okay to drive?"

"Guess I shouldn't have had that extra glass of wine on a work night, but what the hell, it's our tenth anniversary. By the way, you outdid yourself. That was the best damned barbequed salmon I've ever had. She leaned over, kissed her partner, and giving her the tulip, headed inside to get her purse and jacket. She stuck her head back out the door. "See you tomorrow at breakfast."

She hadn't told Liz or any of their friends that she was making a special piece to honour Kaydee and Edda. It would be hung in the dining area of the church basement, where the ladies had spent so much time.

∼

Trish hurried down the main hall of the mushroom farm heading for the locker room. Passing the open door to the supervisor's office, she stuck her head in.

"Hey, Greg. How's it going?"

He glanced up from his desk. "Hi, Trish. Hey, why did the mushroom get invited to all the parties around town?"

"I know this one," she said laughing, "because he's a fungi!" She continued down the hall shaking her head—Greg and his corny jokes.

Once inside the locker room, she grabbed a pair of clean coveralls from the bin by the door and picked a hairnet out of the carton. After dialing in the combination to her locker, she stuffed her jacket, purse, and running shoes inside, then put on her coveralls, hairnet, and grabbing her hard hat, left the room.

She didn't have a problem following the hygiene and safety rules—no long fingernails, no nail polish, no perfume, no food, and no jewelry. The only jewelry she ever wore was her championship soccer ring. During her glory days on the high school soccer team, they had won the Ontario-wide championship, and each player received a silver ring to honour the event.

She was halfway down the hall when she noticed she was still wearing it. Instead of wasting time going back to her locker, she slipped it off her finger and stuck it in her pocket. Further down the hall, she checked out the work schedule posted on the wall to see what cell (a dingy growing room) she would be working in and with who. Only two people worked each cell on the nightshift, and this night it appeared her cellmate was Dylan Chadwick.

Unlike conventional farming, mushroom farming was year-round, with harvesting three times per day. Except for the forklift's whine and beeping, the night shift was quiet compared to the hustle and bustle of the busy day shift. She waved to a fellow harvester entering a grow room on the far side of the loading dock as she made her way to cell number nine. These growing rooms—cells—were the dark and humid incubators that mushrooms loved.

Bacteria was spread easily to the mushrooms, so a disinfectant foot bath was located just inside the door. After dipping the soles of her boots in the solution, she grabbed a trolley cart containing a weigh scale, plastic bins for size sorting, and an orange-handled knife from the bucket nearby. She was all set.

SILENCE IS ~~GOLDEN~~ DEADLY

She was always impressed by how fast the fungi grew. It took only two weeks for mushroom pins to form after planting, and then they grew fifty percent per day—pretty amazing! Soon the large wooden grow-boxes were blanketed with delicate white balls called the first flush, ready for picking. In another five to six days, the second and third flush appeared. The room was eight feet wide by twenty feet long with two long rows of wide wooden boxes, three rows high. The newer mushroom farms had aluminum shelving, while this farm, at least twenty years old, still had the old, heavy-duty wooden shelving and growing boxes. It did have overhead lighting though, not like in years past when pickers had to wear headlights attached to their hard hats.

It appeared Dylan was already here, perched high above the floor on the metal hydraulic lift platform. It moved up and down, right and left, allowing pickers to reach the wooden boxes along the top two rows.

"Hey, Dylan. How's it going?" she called out.

She heard a mumbled response from above as she grabbed a pair of plastic gloves from the bin, snapped them on, and started picking. Gently picking three mushrooms at a time, she delicately twisted them off their stalks, being careful not to bruise or damage the caps. With the knife, she snipped the ends off, tossing them into the waste bucket attached to the side of each growing box. After sorting the mushrooms by size and grade, she put them into their respective plastic bins, then weighed each basket when it was full.

With her wireless earbuds in place, she listened to Shania Twain's hit songs and hummed along. Her back was sore from gardening the previous day, so she took a break, and putting her hands on her hips, she closed her eyes, leaned back, and stretched.

Something tickled her cheek— thinking it was a fly, she waved it away. She was surprised a fly would have gotten in with all the stringent precautions. Then, she felt it again. Reaching up, her fingers touched what felt like it a piece of wire dangling from the hydraulic lift above. She grabbed at the wire, but with her gloves on, she couldn't quite grasp it.

What the hell was this!

Still looking up, the wire slipped down over her head and around her neck.

She quickly pulled the gloves off reaching for the wire, the knife cluttering to the ground. Shocked at the sound of the lift kicking into gear, she panicked as the platform began to rise. The wire immediately began tightening.

Realizing what was happening—her eyes grew wide with terror. Then as her feet lifted off the ground, the wire became so tight she couldn't get her fingers under it. She clawed frantically at it, her nails digging deep into her neck, leaving long, bloody gouges as the wire sank deeper and deeper into her soft, doughy flesh. She hung there unable to breathe, blue tongue hanging out—kicking and squirming. It didn't take long for her head to feel like it was about to explode. Her eyes protruded like a pop-eyed guppy. Her bowels finally let go, then blackness.

CHAPTER TWENTY-TWO

Brynn

(Saturday, June 23)

I WAS RUNNING LATE and was almost out the front door when the phone rang. Sam shuffled out of the kitchen wearing his white T-shirt and yellow smiley-faced boxers. "I'll get that," he said, grabbing the phone in the living room. Chewie followed along behind waiting to be fed, stuck to his heels like a piece of old chewing gum. Sam held his hand over the mouthpiece, "It's Liz."

I frowned, then whispered, "Tell her I'll call her back."

His hand still covering the mouthpiece, he held the phone out towards me. "She sounds upset."

I hurried back in, almost tripping over the dog and took it. "Hi Liz, what's up?"

"Trish never made it home this morning. Have you heard from her?"

"No, sorry, I haven't."

"She always comes home right after her shift. I can't imagine where she could be. I called the mushroom farm and spoke to a supervisor, but he wasn't working the shift last night. He went and checked to see when she had clocked out. Two o'clock is all he could tell me. So, where can she be?"

"Could she have come home and gone out again?"

"There's nothing open in town at that hour, and she's always tired after work, comes home, and goes straight to bed. Her side of the bed hasn't been slept in."

"There's got to be a reasonable explanation." I looked over at Sam.

He mouthed, "Check the hospital".

"She's only been gone for a few hours, but if you're worried, you might check the hospitals. I don't want to scare you, but she could've had an accident on the way home."

"Oh geez, I hadn't thought of that. Lord have mercy!"

"Now Liz, don't get yourself in a panic; Trish could walk through the door any minute."

"I hope so."

"I was just leaving for work. I'll stop by the mushroom farm on my way and see what I can find out. I'll call you as soon as I get back to the pantry."

Dark grey clouds floated overhead as I approached the sprawling Hillcrest Mushroom Farm—the dark grey building matching the sky. I noticed the smell was quite bearable today. At times the composting manure got so foul-smelling it made one's eyes water. I wondered how people living nearby could stand it on bad days. In the heat of the summer, with no breeze, they probably couldn't open their windows, barbeque, sit on their patios, or send their children out to play in the backyard.

After parking my car, I looked around for Trish's beige Toyota Corolla. Not seeing it anywhere, I continued inside. No one was in the main office, so I headed down the corridor and stopped at the first open door, poking my head in.

"Can I help you?" A deep voice behind me asked.

Startled, I turned around to find a short, heavy-set man, in jeans and a blue-checked shirt, staring at me from under a blue hard hat. A hairnet covered his black hair and beard.

"I was looking for the supervisor."

"You found him," he said, smiling. "How can I help?"

I noticed the name tag on his shirt. "Mr. Larson, I called earlier about a friend who worked the late shift and hasn't come home yet. She should've been home hours ago. We're getting worried. We were told she clocked out at 2:00 a.m."

"Yes, I believe you called earlier asking about a Trish Fox? I've seen her around, but she doesn't usually work my shift. Follow me; we can check the schedule and see who was working with her last night." We headed down the hall and stopped in front of a large whiteboard on the wall, with names, dates, and times filled in with black magic marker. "Dylan Chadwick," he said.

"Oh, I know Dylan," I said. "I'll give him a call."

"I wish I could be of more help. I can give you the name and number of the supervisor on duty last night. He's probably asleep right now, so he won't appreciate being disturbed. I'd wait a couple of hours before calling him."

He wrote the man's name and number down on a piece of paper and handed it to me." After thanking him, I asked if there was a locker room, and if so, could I have a look? "Maybe something there will give us a clue."

He nodded. "Sure, don't see why not; follow me."

There was a supply of hairnets in a large box by the door as we entered. Grey metal lockers lined both sides of the room, and I could see a washroom down back. Most of the lockers had locks on them. "Do employee have assigned lockers—and do you have a record of their combinations?"

"Workers usually use the same locker and are responsible for bringing their own locks. Only they know the combination. He pointed to a sign over the door: *Management is NOT responsible for anything missing or stolen.*"

"We try to keep a record," he said. "I'll go check."

While he was gone, I called Liz to get the combination to Trish's locker.

The phone was snatched up on the first ring. "Oh, it's you." She sounded disappointed. "I thought it might be Trish."

I was sorry to hear Trish wasn't back yet. I told her I was at the mushroom farm, and asked if she knew the combination to Trish's locker.

After a pause—"No, sorry, I don't, and I don't know any of her PINs either."

I'd just hung up when Supervisor Larson returned to the room. "Her locker number is twenty-nine," he said. As he came through the door, I noticed a camera over the door. Pointing to it, I asked, "Is it possible to check the video camera?"

He crossed his arms, eyes rolling upward, thinking. "I can't do it right now, but maybe in a couple of hours I'll have time. I'll check it out and give you a call."

Not wanting to push my luck, I hesitated before asking. "Her partner didn't know the combination. Do you think you could... um, saw through the lock?"

"What?" He squinted at me, then—"Uh, okay, as long as I'm not held responsible for destroying property."

"No worries. This is important."

The supervisor disappeared again. When he came back, he was carrying a bolt cutter. It didn't take long for him to cut through the lock shackle and open the locker door.

There was nothing inside the locker except her work boots. No jacket, street clothes, running shoes, purse, or phone. "Looks like she changed and left," I said.

The supervisor looked at his watch. "Sorry, gotta get back, the next shift will be starting soon."

As I was leaving the room, I took a quick look around and saw a small, flat piece of metal on the floor, just under her locker. I went back, picked it up with a tissue from my purse, and put it in my pocket.

CHAPTER TWENTY-THREE

Brynn

(Saturday, June 23)

AFTER ARRIVING AT THE Pantry, I flipped the sign on the door over to "Open" and went straight to the back and put the coffee on. While it was brewing, I pulled out my phone and called Liz. "Any news yet?"

"No—nothing! I've called everyone I can think of, including the hospitals. No one has seen or heard from her. What about you?"

I relayed the little I had learned at the mushroom farm and told her I had the number of the supervisor who worked the night shift. I'd call him as soon as we hung up. I'd also call Dylan Chadwick, as he was the one working with Trish last night.

The distress in Liz's voice was building, "I just don't get it—where can she be?"

"Liz, try to stay calm. She's only been missing a few hours. I'll make those calls right now and get back to you." I hung up.

I grabbed my favourite mug from the shelf above the coffee-maker, the one with the photo of Chewie on it—a Mother's Day gift from my fur baby—and poured myself a much-needed cup of caffeine. Then, I pulled out the piece of paper with the supervisor's number and dialled it. It was quickly answered by a woman's quiet voice.

"May I speak to a Greg Morrison please?" I asked.

"He's sleeping right now. Can I take a message?"

"I'm sorry," but this is important. I wouldn't have bothered you otherwise. I was told he worked the late shift at the mushroom farm last night. Trish Fox, an employee who worked that shift has gone missing, and her family and friends are worried sick. I'm hoping maybe he can shed some light on where she might be. Maybe she mentioned where she was going to him, or he saw her leaving with somebody? Anything really. We haven't gone to the police yet, but that's our next step."

"Hang on a minute," she said.

I took another sip of my coffee and waited. Finally, a man's raspy voice answered. "Hello? Can I help you?"

"I'm so sorry to bother you Mr. Morrison, but as I told your wife, a friend of ours, Trish Fox, is missing. Did she say anything to you about where she might be going after work? Did you see her leave? Was she with anyone?"

"Well, I saw her when she came in. She always sticks her head into my office. But that was the only time I saw her. All the workers left when the shift ended. I always check the picking rooms before leaving and didn't see anyone.

"If you do remember anything, would you call me? I thanked him and once again apologized for waking him up.

Then I dialed the Chadwicks' number. Betty answered.

"It's Brynn, Betty. I know it's early, but I need to speak to Dylan."

"He's sleeping."

"It's rather urgent; could you wake him up, please? I wouldn't ask if it wasn't important."

There was a pause, then, "I'll try."

Just then, the front doorbell tinkled an arrival. Sophie entered the store wearing a red plaid sweater with a picture of a large, black Scottie dog on the front. It was the first time I thought… she actually looked her age. Normally, she stood tall—all four feet, eleven inches of her. But, today as she walked down the aisle towards me, her shoulders sagged and there were dark circles visible under her eyes When she reached me, I noticed the sparkle, usually seen in them, was missing. I took another sip of coffee, and pointed toward the pot. "Coffee's fresh, Sophie. Have a cup."

After holding the phone for what seemed like forever, Dylan finally came on the line. "Hello?"

"Hi, Dylan. Sorry to wake you. It's Brynn Grant. We're trying to find Trish Fox who is missing. You worked with her on the late shift at the mushroom farm last night, right?"

"Don't know how I can help. Didn't go to work last night."

"But your name is on the schedule next to hers."

"Yeah. I was supposed to go to work. But I got a call from the office saying not to bother coming in—said they didn't need me."

"Who's they, and did they say why?"

"Someone from the office. Look, I don't know nothin'. I gotta go." The phone went dead.

I scratched my head, puzzled, then looked over at Sophie and changed the subject. "Did Liz call you?"

She nodded. "Poor dear. She's beside herself with worry. Is there any news yet?"

"That was Dylan on the phone just now. He was supposed to have worked with Liz last night but, said he didn't go in. So, who was she working with? I think it's time for Liz to file a missing person report. I'll go with her for moral support. Sophie, could you watch the Pantry until Lori-Anne gets in?"

"Dunna ye worry, lass," she said, waving her hand. "It's no bother; just go."

∽

Liz was already pacing back and forth at the top of her driveway when I arrived to pick her up. She slid in to the passenger's seat beside me. "I thought I'd have to wait forty-eight hours to file a missing person report," she said. "That's what they say on all the police shows. But, when I called the station, the officer said there's no such policy. They look at each case individually."

"Good. So, the police know we're coming?"

"Uh-huh. Boy, if Trish has gone somewhere without telling me and doesn't have a good explanation—I mean really good explanation," she scowled, "I'm gonna kill her!"

We entered the station, sidling past two burly police officers headed in the opposite direction. Nearing the front desk, I could see the name tag on the officer behind the counter.

"Hello, Officer Laduc. Is Chief Boyd in today?"

"He's out right now. He'll be back later this afternoon. Can I help?"

"I hope so," I said, glancing at Liz. This is my friend Elizabeth Jenkins. She would like to file a missing person report."

His attention turned toward Liz. "Yes, you called a little while ago, I believe. Who's missing again?"

"My partner, Patricia Fox. She didn't come home after working the night shift at the mushroom plant. She's usually home around 2:30 in the morning. It's now—she looked at her phone—1:00 p.m. No one has seen or heard from her. I've checked everywhere, including the hospitals, to make sure she wasn't in an accident. I'm worried," she said, rubbing her hands together.

A phone ringing drew the officer's attention away from us, and he excused himself to answer it.

Liz stood there, tense, fidgeting with a gold cross on a chain around her neck.

"It's going to be okay," I said, giving her a quick hug.

Officer Laduc came back. "She's only been missing a few hours. If she were a missing child, that would be a different story."

"But this isn't like her," Liz said, her voice rising. "She has a routine. After work she's home by about 2:30 a.m. There's nothing open around town that late, not even the bars. So, she wouldn't go anywhere. Once she's home she might have a quick snack, then goes to bed."

SILENCE IS ~~GOLDEN~~ DEADLY

"Okay, if this situation isn't normal, by all means file a report."

"Good!" I said. "Where do we start?"

The officer pulled out papers and a clipboard from under the counter and handed them to Liz with a pen. "Fill out the missing person report, and we'll need a recent photo of the missing person."

Liz rummaged around in her purse and found a head-and-shoulders shot of Trish in her wallet. "Here's one," she said handing it to him.

"Excellent, we'll put that with the report. You can fill the report out in there." He pointed to a small, quiet room with a desk and two chairs. When you're finished, just give me a shout."

After finishing the report, I asked Officer Laduc to notify Chief Boyd and have him phone me as soon as possible.

I was dropping Liz off at home when his call came through. When the call was over, I looked at Liz. "It seems the chief is taking this very seriously. He's on his way over to the mushroom farm now to check the security cameras. He also wants to come by and have a look at Trish's computer . . . see if anything relevant shows up. He's asked us to make a list of all her family, friends, and acquaintances with their phone numbers, and he's talking about arranging a search party if she's not back soon.

"Oh, God." Her lips trembled. "Maybe he thinks something bad has happened to her."

"I think it's just Charlie doing his job," I said, trying to ease her mind. I gave her a quick smile and a hug for reassurance.

However, I couldn't help the sinking feeling in the pit of my stomach.

CHAPTER TWENTY-FOUR

Dylan

(Saturday, June 23)

FROM UNDER HIS PILLOW, Dylan's phone jumped to life, belting out "OMG" by Usher. He grabbed the phone and pushed himself up, and his eyes brightened when he saw who the caller was. "Prissy?"

"Hey, are you ready to go?" She asked.

"Huh? Go where?" He said flicking the hair out of his eyes. "Um, you broke up with me, Pris, remember?"

"You moron. Whatever gave you that idea? I've been busy planning our trip. Then, I couldn't find my bloody cell phone. Can you believe it *she* took it! Lara. I found it in her purse when I was—you know—lightening her wallet this morning. I can't use the house phone. She listens to everything. I wouldn't be surprised if she has it bugged. If she catches me talking to you now, she'd freak out. I didn't get a chance at the teacher's funeral to tell you what's been going on. She won't let me out of her sight."

SILENCE IS ~~GOLDEN~~ DEADLY

"I haven't seen you at school. Where have you been?" Dylan asked.

"I'm ready to blow school off. Nothing gets done after exams, anyway. Besides, I've been busy getting ready for our trip: bought our bus tickets, went to the bank and got some U.S. cash, and had to buy clothes and shoes. Got those fake nails—you know, the kind that my friend Tara has, right? We're leaving tomorrow afternoon. Are you ready?"

He was speechless.

"*So*, are you coming? I'm going whether you go or not!"

Stunned at first, he then gave a bark of laughter. "You'd have to nail my feet to the floor to keep me here!"

"Good, I'll meet you—"

A knock on his bedroom door interrupted his conversation as his mother poked her head inside. "Hold on a second," he said, then, yelled out—"*What?*"

Worry creased his mom's face. "There's a police officer downstairs who wants to talk to you."

"Me? Why?"

"How should I know? Go find out, he's waiting in the hall."

"Gotta go Pris, I'll call you back." He stuck his phone in his pocket, then followed his mother downstairs, where Officer Laduc was waiting.

"What? Am I in trouble? I haven't done anything."

"We just need to ask you some questions down at the station. That's all. It won't take long."

At the station, the officer led Dylan into a small interrogation room. "The Chief will be with you shortly," he said, closing the door behind him. Dylan scanned the room, then flopped down in the chair in the corner. Minutes later, Chief Boyd came through the door and asked him if he wanted a drink. Water? Pop? Coffee?

Dylan asked for a Red Bull.

"Red Bull? You think we've got that stuff around the station?" he snorted, then went back out to see what he could find.

Dylan, meanwhile, sat there leaning forward, head down, hands clasped together in his lap. Then straightening up, he tossed his head back and looked around the room. Except for a desk with a chair behind it and a light fixture hanging from the ceiling, the room was bare. When he noticed a small video camera tucked up in a corner of the room, he couldn't resist making a cross-eyed fish face at it. His hands fluttering on either side of his head like gills. Then, with a start, like being jabbed in the ass with a pin, he remembered he was supposed to call Prissy back. Lifting his butt off the chair, he wriggled the phone out of his back jeans pocket.

"Hi Pris, you'll never guess where I'm at." He waited a second then—"the police station!"

"*What?*"

"They want to ask me about a missing person who works at the mushroom farm."

He could hear someone fidgeting at the door.

"Gotta go call you later." Lifting his butt again, he wedged the phone into his back pocket.

Chief Boyd elbowed his way through the door carrying a can of coke in one hand and juggling a steaming cup of coffee in the other. After putting his coffee down on the desk, he handed the coke over to Dylan. "Sorry. No Red Bull."

Dylan took the can, snapped the tab, took a gulp and slouched back down in the chair.

"Were you working at the mushroom farm last night?"

"No."

"You were scheduled to work alongside Trish Fox. How do you explain that?"

"I got a call from the office telling me not to bother coming in.

"Do you know who called you?"

"No. Said they had enough pickers and didn't need me. I'm quitting anyway, so why should I give a shit?"

Chief Boyd peered over the steam rising from his cup. "I'm surprised your parents let you work on school nights."

"Well, I'm eighteen; I can do what I want. I usually work the evening shift on Fridays. Sometimes on Wednesdays as well."

"Why are you quitting?"

"There's no reason for me to stick around here, so I've decided to leave. Maybe go to California," he said, sliding further down in the chair, crossing his arms and legs.

"Well, that may be so, but I think you should stick around for a while. We might need to talk to you again."

"I don't know why? Like I said, I don't know nothin, I wasn't there."

"Is there anyone who can vouch for your whereabouts last night?"

"I was up in my room all night. My mom was home, but she's out of it these days since Trevor—well, you know—so she wouldn't know or care where I was."

"Yes, but did anyone actually *see* you last night?"

His face screwed up thinking, then, "Oh, yeah, my dad's back. I saw him lying on the couch and told him I wouldn't be going to work."

"What time was that?"

"Well, I went into the kitchen to heat-up a burrito and take it back to my room, so I guess it was round 5:00."

"We've checked the video camera footage at the farm. The camera over the front entrance shows an unidentified person entering the building with a group of employees. The person is wearing a hoodie pulled down over their face. There are cameras throughout the plant—in the locker room, growing rooms, and cafeteria, and this person doesn't appear in any other footage. We think someone might have intentionally disabled the camera in the cell where you were supposed to work with Trish Fox."

"I don't know how many times I have to tell you—I wasn't there!"

"Okay, Dylan." Chief Boyd stood up, went to the door, and swung it open. We're finished here for the time being, but that California trip will have to wait. Stay put."

CHAPTER TWENTY-FIVE

Brynn

(Monday, June 25)

I SAT RIFLING THROUGH my wallet for the correct change at the Tim Horton's drive-through, when I heard talking and laughing. It surprised me when I looked up to see Seymour Harding and his secretary, Bunny Benoit, walking past the drive-through lane.

I did a double take when I saw him slap her ample derriere and squeeze it before giving it a couple of playful pats. They didn't seem concerned about who might be watching.

Bunny giggled girlishly, slapping his hand away. "*You big dipstic*k!"

For the first time ever, I actually felt sorry for his wife, Lara. She must know about his roving eyes, and hands—most people did. Unable to turn away, I stared, mesmerized. But by the time I paid for my coffee and looked back up, they were gone.

I arrived at the Pantry well after 1:00 p.m. Sophie was there busy talking to Betty Chadwick, who had her daughter in tow.

"Hi, Betty," I said, smiling down at Deedee. Shy as always, the little girl turned, and grabbing her mother's leg, buried her face in the folds of her long skirt. I was pleased to see Betty looking healthier than she had in a while. Her face was no longer drawn, and her honey-blonde hair was trimmed and tidy, with no dark roots showing. "It's good to see you, Betty. How are you feeling?"

"Much better. I just stopped by to thank you all for your help during the last couple of weeks. I don't know how I would've managed without it." A look of discomfort crossed her face. "I'm so sorry to hear about your friends' deaths."

A car engine starting up in the driveway.

Betty looked out the door. "A volunteer from the Hospital Auxiliary is driving us to Kingston for Deedee's first round of treatments," she said. "I guess we'd better be going." After prying her daughter loose from her skirt, she grabbed the child's hand, and headed for the door.

"Hold on just a second," I called after her. Hurrying back, I grabbed a few oatmeal/raisin cookies from the cooling tray, and put them in a paper bag. Then, rushing back, I handed them to her. "These are for the trip," I said, rubbing the little girl's curly head.

On her way out the door, she turned, "By the way, Joe's back. I was surprised to see him sleeping on the couch this morning."

We waved goodbye as they left.

Through the window, Sophie and I watched as they climbed into the car and drove away.

"Nice to see Betty doing better," Sophie said. "Is there any news about Trish?"

"Nothing yet, but Charlie is doing everything he can to find her." I glanced at the Felix the Cat clock on the wall, its googly eyes sliding left and right in unison with the tick-tock of its swinging tail. It was 2:00 p.m. "We better organize a group to start making missing person posters, and have the posters distributed around the county. I'll contact the radio station, if the police haven't already, to make sure they announce a missing person's bulletin on the news. I'll let the police know what we're doing. Maybe there's something else they can suggest. The Chief said, if we don't hear any news by tomorrow, he'll start organizing a search party."

~

Two days passed, and there was still no sign of Trish. Friends, associates, and church volunteers had missing person signs with the smiling face of red-headed Trish posted all over the county and surrounding areas.

Liz couldn't eat and was downing tranquilizers like candy, sleeping half the day. I was over at her house making her a lunch anyway when her kitchen phone rang. I picked it up and carried it out into the hall. It was Charlie asking how Liz was doing.

"Not well," I said quietly, so she wouldn't hear. Did you want me to get her?"

"No, don't disturb her. But let her know we are organizing a search party tomorrow. The trail is cold inside the mushroom farm. It's time to do a wider search of the area. I was thinking you and your friends might want to participate.'

"Of course, we certainly will. Just tell us what to do."

"The police will be at the west-end parking lot at the mushroom plant. We're asking volunteers to meet there at 7:00 a.m. sharp. We're getting help from the Fire Department, along with the Lions and Rotary Clubs. If you can think of anyone else who might want to help, ask them. But we don't want to see anyone under eighteen come out. We don't know what we might find. We shouldn't expose children to anything, well..."

"I get it. Is there anything else I need to know?"

"Ask everybody to wear long pants and sleeves, a hat, good shoes, no sandals. They could be walking through swampy areas. Bring a phone, walking stick and whistle. We'll supply bottled water. We'll give more directions after everybody arrives."

"Thanks, Charlie. I'll get the word out."

"If I can't make it out there tomorrow in time, Officer Laduc will be in charge. We're expecting a large turnout. But more is always better. Good luck."

I hung up and went back into the kitchen. Liz sat at the table wearing a housecoat and socks, hair looking like she had just gotten out of bed. "Who was that?"

I explained about the search party being organized for tomorrow.

"Good, it's about time," she said, straightening up. "Count me in."

"I don't think that's a good idea, Liz. It's going to be a stressful, tiring day."

Her eyes glossed over and her chin raised in defiance. "Just try to stop me!"

I opened my mouth to argue, but stopped. "Okay, I said, putting my arm around her. If you feel that strongly, of course. We'll go together."

CHAPTER TWENTY-SIX

Brynn

(Monday, June 25)

THERE WAS NOTHING ELSE to do but fess up. I *had* to confide in Sam. I felt sick not having told him what our woman's group did. My husband is the most honest person I know. I didn't tell him—because he wouldn't understand the altruistic reason our group did what we did. But the unimaginable has happened, two dead and one missing—a matter of life or death. I knew what he would say, and braced myself for the inevitable shocked look of horror on his face when he learned the truth. Would he ever trust me again?

Tired both physically and emotionally, I wasn't in the mood for making dinner, so I stopped in at the China Garden Restaurant and ordered a couple of Cantonese Chow Mein dishes to go.

I was just getting the takeout bag from the back seat of the car when Sam pulled his car into the driveway behind me. He took the bag from me and gave me a kiss. As we entered the house, Chewie, our little barking jumping-jack, greeted us excitedly at the door.

"I could do with a drink before dinner," Sam said. "What about you, Hon? Would you care to join me?"

"Yes, I would." *No need to ask me twice I thought.* "How about you take Chewie out for a walk and a pee, and I'll make the drinks?"

I heard the back door close behind him as I made my way to the liquor cabinet, pulled the gin bottle out and got two glasses down from the cupboard. I made myself a drink, hoping it, would help give me that extra boost of courage I needed to finally confess. Then waited for his return.

When he and Chewie returned, I made him a drink, and then, after finishing our meal, we sat on the couch. Sam's arm wrapped around my shoulders. Sipping on my second drink, I was ready.

Half way through my confession, he took his arm away, and leaning forward put his head between his hands, eyes closed, his head shaking like a bobble-head doll.

He looked at me. "Geez, Brynn! I'm not sure what to say! Not telling me is one thing, but not telling the police? What were you thinking? He stared at me like he didn't know who I was. Gulping down the rest of his drink, he leaned back on the couch, his face like stone.

I couldn't speak.

He tapped the side of his glass. I could tell he was thinking—his head still shaking. "You know you'll have to go to the police first thing in the morning and tell Chief Boyd everything you've just told me." Once again, he closed his eyes, then, opening them, looked at me. "It's going to be hard to make a case against Seymour since the only eyewitness, Edda, is gone. And Seymour must have had his car repaired by now. He'll say the money he gave you was a church donation. At least, if that's the case, you won't be charged with blackmail." He took a giant breath and let it out slowly. "I'm worried because even though Edda withheld evidence from the police, you and the other women could be in deep trouble for keeping quiet. Accomplices to the fact. A lie by omission is still a lie. I know you meant well, Brynn . . . but, really!"

My cheeks were burning; I felt like a child being scolded. "We thought taking the money was the right thing to do. And, we didn't lie—we just didn't tell all we knew. Everybody has done that from time to time."

"But Brynn, what you neglected to tell, has had dire consequences." His sad eyes looked heavy with worry.

"I'll go to the police station first thing in the morning." I stood there as tears welled in my eyes and feelings flooded through me—sadness, remorse. I offered him my hand. "I'm so sorry, Sam."

Drained from my long, emotional day, I decided to call it a night. "I'm heading to bed, how about you?"

"I don't know if I *can* sleep," he said, standing up and looking at me, a strained smile on his face. "I know your heart was in the right place," he said, taking my hand and giving it a squeeze.

We made our way upstairs to the bedroom. Chewie, sound asleep on the living room rug, seemed to have a sixth sense and immediately jumped up and trotted after us.

∽

The following morning, I phoned Georgie to let her know Sophie and I were off to the police station to tell all.

When we arrived at the station, Officer Aaron Laduc was sitting at his desk behind the counter, shuffling papers.

"Officer, is the chief in?" I asked, shoulders back, trying to feel *and look* confident. But, I felt like my younger self in school, heading to the principal's office and waiting to be reprimanded. Clearing my throat, I spoke up. "It's very important we speak to him,"

He nodded. "I'll check." He called through to the chief's office. "Says, he has a few minutes to spare before his next meeting." Coming out from behind the counter, he held the door open for us. "Follow me."

"No need, laddie," Sophie said. "We know the way."

Charlie was at his desk, flipping through papers. We tapped on the open door. He glanced up and waved us in.

"So, what can I do for you?" His gaze shifting from Sophie to me as he straightened his papers.

I started recounting the details of Edda recognizing the logo on Seymour's car and the visit we made to confront him at the plant.

Charlie had stopped shuffling his papers, and was now sitting back in his leather chair, hands clasped across his belly, mouth a grim line, studying us.

"I'm surprised at you ladies, honestly I am. You know, I could charge you with withholding evidence, obstruction of justice, blackmail or any number of things. Lucky for you, the blackmail charge probably wouldn't stick, depending on what Seymour Harding has to say about the cheque. Do you realize that by not telling us about the logo sooner, important evidence involving the Harding's vehicle will be long gone?" He sighed, staring at us. "Considering the only eyewitness is gone, your accusation will be hard to substantiate." He sat there just shaking his head.

Afraid now to hold anything back, I told the Chief that Sophie and I had gone over to the Oldenbergs' place to scout things out ourselves. "It's hard to believe that Kaydee would even set foot in a house with cats; much less end up trapped in a room full of them." I looked at him, then pulled three baggies from my purse and put them down on his desk. "At the Oldenbergs', we found a crumpled, empty cigarette pack and a smashed piece of black plastic, and I found this small piece of metal on the floor under Trish's locker at the mushroom farm."

Charlie sighed. "Leave the investigating to us. I can't stress this enough. You could get hurt." His eyes bore into us as he leaned forward—"*Do you understand?*" We nodded. He hit the intercom button and asked Officer Laduc to escort us out and take our statements.

CHAPTER TWENTY-SEVEN

Lara

(Tuesday, June 26)

LARA'S HOUSEKEEPER HAD TAKEN the afternoon off, a huge inconvenience for her. Nursing a toothache, Mrs. Patterson had gone to the dentist after lunch, leaving Lara to finish making the fancy sandwiches herself. It was her turn to host her Society of Women Engineers monthly get-together (otherwise known as the bitch session). She'd cut off the crusts and arranged the salmon, egg salad, and roast beef sandwiches on the glass platter, with date squares, scones, and cookies stacked on a three-tiered silver platter. Thank goodness, Mrs. Patterson had baked last week. The basement freezer was full of tasty treats. Otherwise, Lara would've had to pull out store-bought baked goods, getting a smirk from her so-called friend Jane Goodwill, who made all her desserts from scratch.

Lara carried a tray of teacups into the dining room just as the doorbell rang. It was a bit early for the women to be arriving. She hoped Seymour would answer it. He had been shut away in his study all morning. Prissy, home from school, was upstairs in her room, probably with her headphones on, so Lara couldn't count on her to get the door.

"Seymour!" She shouted, arranging colourful napkins around the table. He knew she hosted this group every third Tuesday of the month, so he was probably making himself scarce. When there was no answer, she stopped fussing with the arrangements and shouted ...

"Seymour! Get the bloody door! I'm busy."

She heard feet trudging down the hall and the front door opening as a slight breeze drift into the living room.

"Well, hello—Charlie, Aaron," Seymour said, jerking his head back in surprise!

Curiosity getting the better of her, Lara strolled over and stood behind her husband, stunned to find Chief Boyd and Officer Laduc standing on the porch looking officious. Their police cruiser parked in the driveway.

Her body tensed. "What's going on?"

"Hello, Lara," Chief Boyd said, tipping the brim of his cap. "We'd just like to ask you folks a few questions if you don't mind. May we come in?"

"What's this about?" Seymour asked.

"It's about the hit-and-run accident two Friday nights ago, resulting in the death of the Chadwick boy."

Seymour's eyes narrowed as he stepped aside and let them enter.

The chief craned his neck looking around. Then, glancing into the living room, he asked, "Do you mind if we sit in there? It will be more comfortable."

The officers took a seat on the couch, while the Hardings sat down on the two wingback chairs opposite.

"I'll cut to the chase, Seymour," the chief said, sliding to the edge of the couch. "We have information that your vehicle—your company car—was involved in the Chadwick boy's hit and run."

Lara stiffened. "What? Someone is trying to pin that accident on us? There are enough people around here upset about the plant closure and are just plain jealous of us."

"I wasn't even in town Friday night," Seymour said, ignoring his wife's comment. "I was on my way to the Wainsville Golf and Country Club for a golfing weekend with Frank Peterson. We took Frank's car."

Officer Laduc removed his sunglasses, stuck them on top of his head then fished a notebook and pen from his shirt pocket. "Have you got Frank's number?"

Seymour rattled it off.

"Well, someone witnessed your husband's car at the scene," Chief Boyd said.

Lara's eyes kept darting to the window, worried the ladies would be at the door any minute. She had to get rid of the police. How would it look, the women driving up and finding a police cruiser parked in their driveway?

"Who is this person? Is it one of those church women?" she snapped.

Charlie raised an eyebrow. "We are still in the process of verifying the facts."

"Do we need to call our lawyer?" Lara eyeballed Seymour, who was staring down at his hands, now tightly clasped together in his lap.

"They're only asking questions, Lara," Seymour said, looking over at her. "We have nothing to hide, so calm down."

Chief Boyd looked over at Lara. "Where were you the night of the accident, Mrs. Harding?"

"I was in Beckford. I play bridge once a month. We take turns hosting, and this month, it was at Kari Tisdale's in Beckford." She shifted in her chair, eyeing Seymour, then continued. "When I was heading home, with it being dark and the visibility poor, I didn't see the deer run out on the road, and I hit it."

Officer Laduc, busy taking notes, stopped writing, jerking his head up as he shot a glance at her.

"Did anyone see this happen? Anyone stop?" The chief asked.

She uncrossed her legs, and adjusted her skirt. "No, there aren't many cars around at that time of night. You know that stretch of road to Beckford . . . it's a shortcut with woods on either side. It never has much traffic on it."

"Was there much damage to the vehicle?" the Chief asked. "After I hit a deer a few years back, I had to pay twelve hundred bucks to have my van repaired."

"Not too bad," Lara answered, again looking out the window. "The Lincoln is solid. Safest car in North America. You can probably drive away after slamming it into a tree. The deer hit the front bumper, but there wasn't enough damage to keep me from driving home. I was lucky. The stupid deer wandered off into the woods; probably dead by now. We've already had the vehicle repaired."

"I'll need the name of the auto body shop, and unfortunately, we'll need to take the car back to the station until we've completed our investigation." Charlie paused, looking around. "Is your daughter home? I wouldn't mind having a word with her as well."

Lara nodded, then, striding over to the bottom of the stairs, she bellowed for her daughter to come down. Prissy emerged at the top of the stairs, hands on hips, giving her mother a piercing stare. "*What*!"

"Just get down here," Lara said, turning and going back into the living room. "Why are you asking us these questions? We weren't anywhere near that hit-and-run accident. We didn't see anything."

Prissy came into the room and stood behind her dad's chair, glancing around uneasily.

Chief Boyd turned toward her. "Where were you the night of the accident?"

"At my girlfriend's. I stayed the night and we watched movies."

"Officer Laduc here will need to take down the name and address of your friend." The chief said. "How did you get there and back?"

Lara jumped in. "I dropped her off on my way to Beckford around 6:00 and picked her up the following morning at 11:00."

The chief stood up to leave. Office Laduc followed his lead. "Well, I guess that's all the questions we have for now."

At the front door, the Hardings were thanked for their cooperation and Seymour was asked for his car keys. Seymour reached in his pocket, withdrew the keys and handed them over to the officer.

"Hopefully, you'll have your car back in a couple of days. If we have any more questions, we'll be in touch." Chief Boyd tipped his hat and they left.

It was then that Lara saw Jane Goodwill's car pull into the driveway, Felicity's van just behind.

CHAPTER TWENTY-EIGHT

Lara

(Wednesday, June 27)

THE NEXT DAY, LARA arrived home exhausted after her killer workout at the Better Butts Fitness Centre. She threw her gym bag into the laundry room and headed for the kitchen. Her personal trainer Rio who described *themself* as non-bindary, preferring the pronoun 'Xe' to he or she, had really put her through the paces today. Appearances mattered, so she went to the gym most days. To Lara, exercise was a holy imperative—must keep the flab at bay—look good for her man. She knew she couldn't keep up with the young chickees in his office, but still—

She looked at her watch. It was late afternoon, and Prissy would be home from school soon, but first, time for a drinkie-pooh. She walked past the massive marble-topped island of her newly remodelled kitchen and headed for the liquor cabinet. She might be a fitness buff, but she wasn't above having a little tipple now and then, these days being a little more *now* than then.

Three months ago, this kitchen renovation was all she cared about. Now, much more critical matters needed her attention. Lara grabbed a glass and headed to the double-wide, built-in, Miele stainless-steel fridge to get ice; poured herself a stiff vodka and downed it. She then poured herself another shot and carried it out into the living room.

She placed the drink on the end table, plopped herself down in the blue velvet French Bonaparte chair, let her hair down, and kicked off her shoes. Although surrounded by opulence, she was miserable. She hardly saw Seymour these days. He was either working late, away on business or golfing with his buddies. She'd be happy when the meat-packing plant finally closed for good and a general manager was hired to run things at the new location. Seymour would have more time for his family. Maybe then they could take a vacation, a real one to somewhere warm and exotic. She understood there was a lot of work involved in closing the old plant and overseeing the construction of the new one, but, still . . . this business was taking its toll on their relationship and finances.

Another vice that she kept well-hidden, even though it was bad for her health and especially her image, was the occasional smoke. She reached into the back of the end-table drawer, and pulled out the pack of Winchester Cigarillos Seymour kept hidden there. She pinched one out of the pack, then headed out to the porch to enjoy it with her drink. Thanks to those busybody church women, Seymour's car had been implicated in that Chadwick boy's death. She smirked—they couldn't prove anything. And at least three of the women were now out of the picture. Another problem was Prissy! What was with her and that Dylan kid, anyway? He was a nobody, just like his family. Prissy was told flat-out time and time again to keep away from that *bastard*.

She had hoped sending Dylan a text from Prissy's phone telling him to get lost might work. She was disappointed it hadn't. But she had tried!

With the last of her drink finished, she stubbed the butt of her smoke out on the railing, then took it into the powder room, and flushed it down the toilet. After swishing her mouth out with Listerine, she made her way upstairs to Prissy's room.

Opening the door, she closed her eyes, shaking her head in frustration at the neon-purple paint on the walls. How could anyone possibly sleep in a room this garish colour? Clothes were strewn around the room, on the floor and piled high on the chair under the window.

Lara stood there, hands on her hips, scanning the room, not sure what she was looking for. She didn't trust that girl but had a feeling something was up, although she wasn't sure what.

After rifling through the dresser drawers and poking around in the closet, she sat down in front of the computer. It was password protected. She entered her daughter's favourite colour, looking at the walls and snickering... I wonder what that could possibly be? She made a few more attempts, including her favourite food—nachos and then gave up. Why waste time? She would never figure out what that crazy girl had in her head when picking passwords. Frustrated, she gave the desk a good swift kick. Pain instantly shot through her foot. She hobbled over to the bed, plopped herself down, and removed her shoe, then began massaging her foot. While inspecting her foot to make sure she hadn't broken a toe, her other foot hit against something hard under the bed. She got down on her knees and lifted the bed skirt. A Suitcase.

She pulled it out, plopped it on the bed, and opened it. It was packed inside with Prissy's clothes, shoes, and assorted paraphernalia.

A folder tucked in the back zippered flap of the lid contained five hundred U.S. dollars and two bus tickets. Prissy's name was on one ticket, while—shit, shit, shit! Dylan Chadwick's name was on the other. Her face burned, and her hands clenched into fists as she hit them against her thighs, muttering profanities to herself.

Upon hearing the front door open, she quickly closed the suitcase, shoved it back under the bed, and hurried downstairs.

Prissy flew past her on the staircase without saying a word.

CHAPTER TWENTY-NINE

Prissy

(Wednesday, June 27)

PRISSY OPENED HER BEDROOM door and stood there. "Goodbye room," she said, looking around, creating a mental picture of it before leaving for good. She couldn't help chuckling to herself. To spite her parents, who said she could paint the walls any colour—except black—Pris had picked "Psychedelic Purple." It had this unique, iridescent quality that glowed in the dark, and her mother hated it. Success!

Lara had bought her this "little girl's" creamy-white bedroom suite when she was eight years old. She remembered how excited she was. But, she had out grown it a long time ago. She was no longer a cute, naive little kid. She was sixteen, an adult now, with her own mind and tastes. A multicoloured striped comforter covered the double bed; a blue stuffed elephant lounged against a mountain of pillows. In bold red lettering, one pillow proclaimed "*I Am Not a Morning Person.*" A computer desk and chair occupied one corner of the room, and just above it, magazine clippings of movie stars were plastered on the wall. Makeup containers littered the top of a mirrored little princess vanity table.

Hunkering down by the bed, she grabbed hold of the suitcase she'd packed the night before, pulled it out, and headed for the door. At the door, she put her suitcase down and turned around for one last look. A smile crept across her face—she was happy to be leaving. Her eyes fell on the cuddly pachyderm and dashing back, she picked it up. After giving Bobo a hug and a quick kiss, she tossed him across the room. Her old life was over! She picked up her suitcase, said "Goodbye room," and left.

At the bottom of the stairs, her mother was waiting for her, arms folded tightly across her chest. Prissy ignored her and headed straight for the front door.

"I don't need to ask you where you're going," her mother piped up. "I saw the suitcase and bus tickets. "

"You were snooping in my room again! Bloody hell! No wonder I can't wait to get away from here."

"Hey," her mother said with a shrug, her palms facing outward. "If that's what you want, I'm not going to stand in your way." Arms now down at her sides, a slight smile on her face, she looked almost normal. "I've even called you a cab. She looked down at her watch. "Should be here in about twenty minutes. Come on, let's not argue. Let's sit down and talk like adults for once before you go." Lara motioned for Prissy to follow her into the living room.

Prissy left her suitcase in the hall by the front door and followed her mother into the living room. She perched on the edge of a chair across from her mother, ready for a quick escape. "I'm not gonna change my mind *Lara!*"

"You're only sixteen. You're classified as a minor. Your father and I are still responsible for you."

"I can take care of myself! You don't need to worry about me. This is what I want."

"And what about that boy? What's with you and him anyway? I don't get it? You know how we feel about the Chadwicks."

"How *you* feel! Why do you hate them so much?"

"We don't hate them. Honey, they're just not our class of people. And Dylan follows you around like a lovesick puppy."

"You're just jealous because Dad doesn't pay any attention to you."

Eyebrows pulled inward, her mother hesitated before speaking, her lips forming a grim line. "Prissy, I didn't want to tell you this, but you leave me no choice. When your dad was in high school, he hooked up with Betty Chadwick. Betty Dunhill, back then. She foolishly got herself pregnant and moved away to Toronto to live with her aunt. When she returned to the county, she had a toddler in tow. A boy."

Prissy stared at her.

"For Christ's sake, Prissy, do I have to spell it out for you? Dylan Chadwick is your half-brother. Leave him alone!"

Prissy threw her head back, letting go a crazed laugh, then sneered at her mother. "You'd say just about anything to get what you want, wouldn't you? Do you know why Dad ignores you?" She stood up. Because you're a bitch and a big, fat liar!" Her cheeks blushed crimson. "He saves his attention for that Bunny woman at work. Everybody knows about their *thing* except you."

The cords in Lara's neck went rigid, and the vein at her temple started its tell-tale throbbing. She got up off the couch, and walking over to her daughter, slapped her across the face. "How dare you! After all we've done for you. You're a spoiled-rotten, egotistical little brat. Do you think I'd let you go anywhere on your own? No way, kiddo!"

The doorbell rang.

Rubbing her cheek, Prissy glared at her mother, then ran from the room. At the front door, she snatched up her suitcase and flung the door open. Two burly men in white coats were standing there blocking her exit. In the driveway, just beyond them, she could see a black van with "Rosehaven Academy: Therapeutic Boarding School for Troubled Teens" painted across the doors.

CHAPTER THIRTY

Dylan

(Wednesday, June 27)

DYLAN WAS READY TO go. His backpack contained all the necessities: an extra pair of jeans, a few T-shirts, socks, boxer shorts, toothbrush/paste, soap, and deodorant. His wallet and cell phone were in this jacket packet, his earphones were slung around his neck, and his sunglasses were on top of his head. And even though the police had told him to stick around, he wasn't worried. His friend told him, unless the police have a court order, they can't make you do squat. They only ask you to stick around for their convenience. If leaving made him look guilty, he didn't care—he had nothing to do with that woman's disappearance.

Prissy was meeting him at the bus station in Beckford at 6:00 p.m. The bus left at 7:00. He checked his cell for the time, it was only 4:30 p.m.. He had plenty of time to walk to the Tim Hortons in town where his friend worked, have a sandwich and an iced-cap and wait for his friend's shift to end. Then his friend would drive him to the bus station in Beckford. Dylan promised Prissy he wouldn't be late. Once he and Pris got to Toronto, they'd get the Wanderu bus, which would take them through the States to L.A.

He sank down on his bed, his backpack at his feet, and looked around the room. Although he was pumped about starting a new adventure with Prissy, he couldn't help feeling he was abandoning his mom. A lump rose in his throat. He figured Ma and the kids would be okay, especially now that money from the church was coming in. They could afford Deedee's operation and a bunch of other things too. His eyes started misting over—he knew he'd miss them. But he wouldn't miss Pa, the drunken pig. Sniffling, he pulled himself together, stood up, and picking up his bag, headed out the door.

Passing by the kitchen, he stole a look inside. His mom was bringing milk and sandwiches to the kids at the table. Baby Arti, propped up in his highchair, was squealing, little hands hitting the tray in front of him and drool running down his chin, eager for his Gerber puree'. Dylan didn't have the guts to go in and say goodbye. He'd call his mother later and let her know he was okay. He didn't want her to worry.

Deedee looked up from eating her peanut butter and jelly sandwich, food smeared around her mouth, and saw him in the doorway. She waved her sticky little fingers at him. He waved back. Then, not wanting to blubber like an idiot, he made a beeline for the door.

As he paced back and forth in the crowded bus station, his jacket and bag sitting on the bench, he kept glancing at the clock above the ticket counter—6:30. Where was she? Was he crazy to count on her? Was she planning to dump him again? Too restless to sit down, he picked his stuff up and headed outside. By the door, his eyes caught sight of a missing persons poster on the wall—short red hair, round face. He recognized the woman he was supposed to have worked with at the mushroom farm. With a shrug, he stepped out into the sunshine.

He looked at the people milling around, trying to find the familiar head of rainbow-coloured hair. Since Prissy had gone from blonde to rainbow (she was always changing her hair colour) she was easy to spot—but he saw no sign of her anywhere.

His throat was dry, his shirt clammy with sweat. What the hell? Where was she?

A taxi pulled into the station, and his heart jumped. This had to be her. He hurried over, trying to see inside the cab, but with its tinted windows, he couldn't tell if it was her. But it had to be, since she never cared about the cost of anything, he figured, it would be just like her to make a grand entrance. The driver got out and held up a large manila envelope with "Dylan Chadwick" written in big, bold letters across it.

"Hey, that's me," he yelled, rushing up to the driver.

"I was told to give this to you," the driver said, handing him the envelope. Dylan quickly ripped it open as the driver climbed back into the cab and drove off. Inside was a bus ticket along with a handwritten note:

> *Something has come up and I can't get away. I want you to go ahead and use the bus ticket. I will meet up with you in L.A. as soon as I can. There's a YMCA in Glendale – go there. Don't worry about me, cause everything is okay—just a little set back. I'll call you when I can. See you soon. Enjoy the trip. Pris.*

Stunned, he stood there watching as people filed out of the station and lined up at the buses outside. His bus #9 pulled up, and the doors swung open. The driver stepped down and started taking tickets from the passengers as they boarded.

Dylan stood there—was this note really from Prissy? Or was it another hoax her mother was pulling? He didn't know what to do. This wasn't the way things were supposed to be. They were supposed to go on the trip together. He had been depending on Prissy's sharp wit, and strong personality to take them on this adventure. Now he was alone! He couldn't decide whether to get on the bus or find out what the hell was going on!

Through the station window, he could see his bus. The driver, foot resting on the bottom step, looked around, checking to see if there were any last-minute stragglers.

Dylan hesitated for a split second, then sprinted over, handed the driver his ticket, and climbed aboard.

CHAPTER THIRTY-ONE

Lara

(Wednesday, June 27)

WHEN SEYMOUR WALKED THROUGH the door around 9:00 that evening, Lara was waiting for him. Even before he had time to set his briefcase down, she shoved a brochure in his face.

"What's this?" he said, flipping it over, barely looking at it.

Lara stared at him unsmiling, face pinched. "You won't believe what that daughter of yours has been up to. I found bus tickets up in her room. Two tickets—one for her and, get this, one for Dylan Chadwick. They were planning on leaving for California this afternoon!" She paused, waiting for his reaction. When he just stood there, a baffled expression on his face, she continued. "She was going to leave no matter what! I'm at my wit's end. She doesn't listen to either of us. The only way I could think of stopping her was to send her away—to a reform school. That should knock some sense into her. So, that's what I've done."

He stood transfixed, staring at her. "What do you mean, that's what you've done?"

She nodded toward the brochure. "She's gone. They came by this afternoon and picked her up. I had no choice. It was either that or she'd run off with *your* son!"

She enjoyed watching his anguish as he struggled to control himself. His shoulders slumped, he closed his eyes, a pained expression on his face. Opening them, he brought the brochure up for a closer look. When he was finished reading, he scratched his head and looked at her like she was certifiable. "How the hell am I supposed to afford this—this boarding school? Nearly six thousand a month! Are you out of your ever-loving mind?"

Her cold gaze fixed on him. "What are we supposed to do? She just turned sixteen: she's still a child! She's about to run away with her half-brother for Christ's sake, and she doesn't even realize it. She's totally out of control. She doesn't listen to us and lies and swears all the time. Even though we could buy her anything she wants, she shoplifts. She hangs out with deadbeats and is failing at school. Hell, I'd be surprised if she has even been going to school! So, what do you want to do, Seymour? Just let our only child flush her life down the toilet? I thought you'd do anything to help her turn her life around."

"Lara, calm down, of course I would, but I can't just crank out money like you think I can. The new plant is behind schedule and we're way over budget. And we both know your darling Daddy's not going to cough up any money."

Silence followed as Lara stood there staring at him, fully aware of how true that was.

She and Seymour had both graduated from Queen's University in Kingston. Seymour took accounting and Lara took bioengineering, following in her father's footsteps. Lara planned to work with her father in the family business and take it over when he retired. But after only three years, she couldn't hack working with her dad. He was a Simon Legree, so she quit. Her father felt let down and never forgave her. However, as Lara was an only child, he gave her and Seymour the start-up money for the meat-packing plant. Upon retiring, her father handed over the company to his business partner, and she and her dad haven't spoken since.

"Same old excuses." Lara said, shaking her head, a tight smile on her face. "I know what's going on. I'm not stupid. I've looked at the books. You've made transfers out of our daughter's trust account that daddy set up for her, for God knows what? I've spoken to a lawyer who says a large amount of that money went to the church recently, and that monthly withdrawals are going out to a condo association in Beckford. What condo? And why would you give that much money to the church? Five hundred thousand dollars. What the hell?" Her eyes bore holes into him. "You're being blackmailed by those church busybodies—aren't you? Well . . . aren't you?"

"Lara please, just listen to yourself."

"No, you listen! And I know all about that little tart at the office. That blonde bimbo, Bunny. You're paying her rent. That's what that condo corporation's monthly payment is all about, isn't it? It doesn't take a genius to figure that out. And what the hell kind of name is that for a grown woman anyway—Bunny? I'll bet she enjoys munching on your big, juicy carrot, huh?"

"Lara. Stop it! That's enough. No wonder our daughter is such a mess, just look at her whacko mother!"

She could feel her heart pounding in her ears, as she spit out. "I don't know where you'll get the money, and I don't care, but you'll pay for our daughter's school and ditch that Bunny broad right away. Let her pay for her own bloody condo. And if I hear you've picked up with her again, I have a lawyer... a shark. We'll take you for every dime. And about those blackmailing church bitches... You have only three of them left to worry about now. You should pray the others have unfortunate accidents too!" Turning on her heels, she marched out of the room.

CHAPTER THIRTY-TWO

Brynn

(Thursday, June 28)

WE ARRIVED AT THE Hillcrest Mushroom Farm early the next morning. The parking lot was already full, and cars lined both sides of the street. I managed to squeeze my car into a parking space, not too far from the building. As we made our way through the crowd, we passed by many familiar faces, including Reverend Jim, along with a large contingent of our fellow church members, including—of all people—Seymour Harding.

"Will ya look oose here!" frowned Sophie, "He's got…"

I nudged her arm and gave a slight nod towards Liz, who was standing beside us close enough to hear. She was already looking extremely distraught. Sophie took the hint and clammed up.

We made our way up to the makeshift wooden platform at the far end of the parking lot and saw Officer Laduc standing there, testing the microphone. After clearing his throat, he addressed the crowd. "Thanks, everyone, for coming out. We are fortunate to have a number of volunteer groups assisting us today. If you are not part of a group that has already submitted names and contact information, please check in with Officer Gunn." He pointed to a female police officer—hands clasped behind her back, elbows out to the sides, planted like a tree in front of the stage. A large map was propped up behind her. She was wearing mirrored sunglasses and looked like a person you wouldn't want to tangle with.

"Officer Gunn will assign you to a group and make sure you have the necessary equipment. The map behind her is marked into grids. After separating yourselves into your group, we'll assign each group a grid area to search. One person in the group will have a walkie-talkie to communicate with an officer. You can then separate into twos or threes but stay at arm's length to the others in your group and maintain a slow steady pace as you look around." He turned toward Officer Gunn. "Do you want to add anything?"

"Be alert at all times," she called out like a drill sergeant. "Look under trees, bushes and in ditches for anything that could point to our missing person. But don't touch anything that could be evidence. Instead, tag it with the red markers we'll give you. Then take a picture of it on your phone and send it to the officer assigned to your group. Hopefully, we can get cell reception out here."

Reverend Jim's hand shot into the air. "What was Trish Fox wearing when last seen?"

Officer Laduc searched his notes. "A blue jacket and jeans."

"And running shoes, black, size 9." Liz called out from the crowd, eager to help.

"Thanks, Liz," Officer Laduc said. "If anyone has any more questions, see Officer Gunn or myself. Good luck!"

After hours of searching a ten-kilometre radius surrounding the mushroom farm, a call went out for volunteers to head back to the parking lot and regroup. Canteens of coffee, hot chocolate and cold drinks, along with boxes of doughnuts, courtesy of the Rotarians, were spread out along a long table. I guided a weary Liz to a seat, then went and got us both a hot chocolate.

Taking a sip of my drink, I looked around and saw Chief Boyd hurrying out of the building. He headed toward Officer Laduc over by the stage. Their heads were stuck together for a few minutes before Chief Boyd turned and started walking toward us.

As he approached, deep circles hung under his eyes, his forehead furrowed as he fished a clear plastic bag out of his pocket and handed it to Liz. "We spent the day searching far and wide, then found this up near the south side of the building, near the compost piles and the large mixer/thrashing machine." He looked at Liz. "Do you recognize this?"

Liz took the bag, turning it over and looking at it, then gasped. "It's Trish's ring."

"Are you sure?" he asked.

She showed him the initials "TF" etched inside the silver band, then swayed, holding her hand up to her forehead. I caught hold of her elbow to steady her. Her voice cracked with emotion. "It's her high school soccer ring. It's the only time Penrith High won the Ontario girls championship. She hardly ever took it off. Maybe at work, but otherwise, she wears it all the time." Her eyes flooded with tears.

I held onto her while eyeing Charlie. "I wonder how it would have gotten there?"

He shook his head, frowning. "We'll find out."

CHAPTER THIRTY-THREE

Seymour

(Thursday, June 28)

SEYMOUR LEANED BACK IN his office recliner at work, stretching his neck and rolled his shoulders. He listened to the constant drumming of rain on the roof. Tieless, top button of his shirt undone and sleeves rolled up, he spent hours hunched over their financial statements. He had sweat checked everything and still couldn't figure out how to pay for their daughter's boarding school. What had Lara been thinking? He reached for the glass of Macallan Highland Scotch Whiskey sitting on his desk beckoning to him. Swirling the amber liquid around, he stared into it, mesmerized. Finally, taking a swig, he looked at the clock—almost 8:00 p.m.

He knew he was in deep shit. Construction on the new meat-packing facility was behind schedule and over budget. The funding he received from the government for building the new plant was almost gone, and the bills were piling up, not to mention his overdue taxes, and, he still hadn't fully paid for the kitchen renovations. Paying for Bunny's condo was a drain, but he wanted to keep her happy. He couldn't afford to lose her; she was the only bright light in his dismal existence. The money he'd forked over to those blackmailing church women was making a bigger hole in his pocket than he'd thought. And to top things off . . . Lara sends their daughter off to that ridiculously expensive Therapeutic Boarding School. What the hell was a "Therapeutic Boarding school" anyway? It wasn't going to cure her. Prissy would always be Prissy. He took another sip. He was surprised his payoff to the church women hadn't worked. But who other than the church women could have mentioned seeing his car?

Just then, the door swung open, and Bunny Benoit appeared in the doorway wearing a sexy, baby-blue, figure-hugging knit dress—leaving little to the imagination.

"Hi, sweetie," she said with a glint in her eye, "how's my sexy dipstick doing?"

He pushed his chair back, waving her over. "Thank God I can count on you, sweetheart. I don't know what I'd do without you. I love you."

She sashayed over to him in her stiletto heels and wiggled down onto his lap, practically purring. "Love you too," she said.

He pressed his face down between her pillowy breasts. She gently raised his chin and, lowering her head, gave him a long, sloppy kiss. When she bobbed up for air, he grabbed her breast and squeezed the nipple.

Her breath was hot against his skin as she whispered in his ear, "Oh, you naughty boy."

His hands on her thighs, he eased her off his lap and stood up. With one arm around her shoulder, he downed his drink and led her over to the couch.

Just as he was busy unzipping his pants, with Bunny laying back on the cushions, her face flushed and eyes sparkling, the phone rang. He ignored it. The ringing finally stopped—then started again. "Geez. Why can't people just leave me the hell alone!" Pulling up his pants, he stumbled over to the desk and grabbed the phone, barking—"What is it!"

"This is Inspector Bagg from Central OPP in Beckford. I'd like to speak to Seymour Cedric Harding?"

"Speaking," he said, lowering his voice to a more professional tone.

"Mr. Harding, sorry to bother you at this hour, but I need to set up a time for you to come down to the station. How does ten tomorrow morning sound? We've got more questions to ask you. It won't take long.

His mouth twisted as he swallowed hard. "What's this about, Inspector?"

"It's about an ongoing investigation we're working on. We'll tell you more at the station."

Although his pulse was racing, he tried to sound nonchalant. "Do I need to bring my lawyer?

"No, I wouldn't think so. We've just got a few questions. But it's up to you. If you think you need a lawyer, by all means, bring one along."

"I'll be there," Seymour said, then hung up. Deep in thought, he glanced over at Bunny, who was waving her index finger at him, a come-hither look on her face. She was either oblivious to the troubling phone conversation he'd just had or wanted to make him feel better.

He pulled the bottle of scotch out of the bottom desk drawer, took a swig, and, carrying the bottle with him, headed back over to the couch.

CHAPTER THIRTY-FOUR

Dylan

(Friday, June 29)

THE BUS PULLED INTO the L.A. terminal located in the industrial area of Los Angeles. Given the rundown conditions of the station and surrounding buildings, Dylan knew these long-haul bus trips were for people like him who couldn't afford to fly or were too frightened. Hey—at least he was here!

At eighteen, he'd had no problem sitting for hours while the bus crossed the Canadian/U.S. border at Detroit, then took historic Route 66 through Illinois, Missouri, Oklahoma, New Mexico, Arizona, and down into California. It was one long, boring journey—taking two and a half days to get here. The bus made no overnight stops. He did feel sorry for the old folks though. He could almost hear their joints creaking when they got off the bus to stretch, have a meal or use the facilities. You'd have to be desperate to use the toilet on board—it reeked of shit. Luckily, he had never been that desperate.

Thank God for his cell phone and earbuds; he could zone out to music or play video games, shutting out all the background talking, hacking, and coughing around him. One old fart sounded like he was about to cough up a lung.

After de-bussing, he wandered over and leaning against a concrete pillar, set his duffle bag down on the station floor beside him. He stood there feeling lost. It brought back memories of the only other trip he ever went on. He was five, and his ma and aunt had taken him to Niagara Falls. Besides the thundering water that shook his tiny bones to the tip of his tiny toes, the thing he remembered most was when he lost sight of his mother. He was panic stricken. That is, until he felt her hand grab his. Then everything was okay. Now, looking at all the people rushing around and the buses coming and going, he felt like that little lost kid again.

He finally stopped a station attendant passing by, and asked for directions to the YMCA.

Soon he was on the city bus taking in the scenery. It left behind the industrial area and headed toward the city centre. Through the cloud of smog, way in the distance, he could just make out the Hollywood sign he'd seen in the movies. As he passed a street called *Avenue of the Stars*, his stomach fluttered with excitement. He kept his eyes peeled looking out the window—maybe he'd see a famous person like Brad Pitt or Taylor Swift walking their dogs or shopping. Boy, that would be something to tell his ma about!

It was a short walk from where the bus stopped to the Glendale YMCA. He entered the old red-brick building and headed through the dimly lit, musty-smelling lobby towards a Mr. Clean look-alike (muscular, bald, and wearing one gold earring) standing behind the front counter.

"This is your lucky day," Mr. Clean said, welcoming Dylan. "A room has just become available—$150 a week. It's yours if you want it. It's on the second floor with a shared bathroom down the hall." He waited for Dylan to make up his mind, then pointed toward a group of young people, huddled together, backpacks on the floor, studying a map. "See that group of kids over there? Just beyond them is a communal room where you can watch TV if you want."

He took the room, then made his way up the stairs to the second floor. The room had a desk, a lamp, chair, and bed. Nothing else. It was dingy, but at least it had a small window overlooking the noisy street below. He checked out the desk drawer. Finding only a tattered Gideon's Bible, he sneered, tossed it back into the drawer and shut it. As a kid, his mom would drag him to church from time to time to attend Sunday School. He didn't mind going because they always had colouring contests. A black-and-white print of a bible story, along with crayons was handed out to the kids. He always won a large chocolate bar for colouring inside the lines, and his prize-winning picture was tacked up on the bulletin board. He felt proud of himself.

Now that he was grown up, he didn't believe in a godly entity. And he never paid any attention to his mother's church-talk nonsense anymore.

Eager to get out and go exploring, he returned to the lobby, picked up a city map, and made his way back to the bus stop. Coming from a small village, the city noise and smells were overwhelming—car horns blaring, taxis tooting, motorcycles revving and weaving through the slow-moving traffic, and scooters flying past on the sidewalks. And the fumes, especially the exhaust from the many busses stopping and starting. No wonder the air was smoggy. And, finding a place to park?

He didn't care if he never owned a car living here, the buses went everywhere. L.A. was overcrowded, overpriced, and polluted—but what it did have was great weather and great opportunities.

He jumped off the bus at Venice Beach and was in awe of the circus of humanity surrounding him—skaters, stoners, artists, street performers. Farther down the long strip of sand, at Muscle Beach, jocks and meatheads were pumping weights, their bodies so huge they looked downright deformed. He chuckled, thinking they probably took a truckload of steroids—shrinking their nuts to the size of M&Ms.

The old hippie culture from his grandparents' era was alive and well at Muscle Beach. A famous Randy's Donuts coffee shop (at least that's what the sign said, World Famous Since 1952) was just ahead, and since his stomach was grumbling, he ducked inside.

Sitting by the picture window spellbound, he watched the Cirque du Soleil of activity out on the boardwalk. The spell was broken when a pretty, young waitress with skinny hips and big tits—probably fake he thought—walked up to his table, her big smile animating her whole face. The name tag on her uniform read "Aurora." After ordering a burger, a Coke and one of their famous donuts, he mentioned he was new in town and asked what there was nearby to see. She started to tell him when a guy at the next table interrupted them, asking for a coffee refill. She returned to his table a few minutes later, offering to show him around when her shift ended in about an hour, if he wanted to wait.

"Sure, that would be dope," he said.

They spent the rest of the day wandering along the boardwalk getting to know each other. As they got acquainted, he discovered she was another wannabe actress waiting tables to pay the bills until her big break came along. They stopped at a fortune teller's tent where an old gap-toothed woman with an inebriated smile and a crooked turban read their fortunes. She said they were both going to become rich and famous. They came out of the tent giggling wishing if only it were true.

"Before we become rich and famous," Aurora said, still laughing, "I can get you a job at Randy's. The busboy just quit. You'll be washing dishes, but at least it's a job. Her eyes flashed at him. "Hey, I've heard they're looking for actors for a new scary, gothic TV series. Since you're tall, good-looking, and with your hair being jet black and shaved off on one side and all—you'd be perfect. You already look the part."

Nobody ever had said he was good-looking before, not even Prissy. A smile tugged at his lips.

"Dylan, what do you think? You wanna try out for a part or what?"

"I'm not an actor."

"Hey, we're all actors when it comes right down to it. Remember Shakespeare's quote—'All the world's a stage, and all the men and women merely players?' Well, they're looking for fresh faces—no previous acting experience necessary. Auditions are next Thursday. I'll be going, and maybe you'd like to tag along? I'll pick up a copy of the audition script and we can look it over together. Nothing to lose. Come on, what do you say?"

He wanted to see Aurora again, so shrugging he said. "Got nothing else to do. Sure, count me in."

For the first time in days, he wasn't thinking about Prissy at all.

CHAPTER THIRTY-FIVE

Georgie

(Friday, June 29)

GEORGIE JUST RETURNED FROM the grocery store and was in the kitchen putting the items away when Hugh rushed in, wearing his yellow Lions Club Jacket with the gold-and-navy crest on the pocket.

"Oh, you're still here?" she said, doing a double take, and glancing up at the clock over the stove. "It's almost 7:00. I thought you'd have left by now. You better get going, or you'll be late."

He bent over and kissed her forehead. "Just leaving. It's been like a revolving door around here since you've left. First Lara Harding came by to pick up a box of books you promised to set aside for the Hospital Foundation's Book-a-Thon. I couldn't remember where you said you put them. She asked for a glass of water, so I asked her in and gave her cold water from the fridge, and she waited in the kitchen while I went looking for the books."

"Sorry," Georgie said, wincing, "I forgot she was coming. I should have told you they were in the garage."

"Well, I eventually found them. She took the books and left. She was barely out the door when her other half showed up helping her collect the books. Guess they got their signals crossed. Seymour stayed for about an hour and we talked about Lion's Club business over a beer."

Georgie winked, giving him the thumbs up. "Wow, lucky you! Two Hardings in one afternoon. How do you rate?"

He grinned, heading for the front door. Then he stopped and turning around, came back and stuck his head in the kitchen. "Oh, you'll be glad to hear Joe Chadwick's out in the laundry room, repositioning the electrical outlets and raising the countertop so your new super-sized washer and dryer arriving tomorrow will fit. "

"I didn't see his truck out front. Has he got his license back?"

"Yup, he parked his pickup out back. He's been working in there for a couple of hours now."

"I hope you didn't give him a beer!"

"Of course not, don't be silly; he's almost finished." Hugh threw her a kiss as he was leaving the room. She could hear the front door's soft thud as the front door closed behind him.

The B&B was fully booked for the long Civic weekend and her thoughts now turned to what needed doing before her guests arrived. The long list tacked up on the fridge was mostly completed. Georgie was well-organized. She already had the guest rooms and the rest of the house cleaned. Now it was time to get busy with the food preparations. Her breakfasts were a hit with her guests, who kept coming back for their delicious French toast, omelettes, cinnamon rolls, and peach scones to die for.

She finished putting the groceries away and turned the gas stove on to preheat. Slipping on her apron, she got all the ingredients and utensils out and set them in an orderly fashion on the kitchen counter. She was ready to start on her pies—apple, and strawberry rhubarb. Nobody knew the secret ingredient in her apple pies was—a splash of brandy. Humming to herself, she went and got the bottle of brandy from the dining room sideboard. Above the sideboard was a beautiful encaustic painting done by Trish. Looking at it, a lump rose in her throat. It was a simplistic picture of a tall glass jar filled with oranges, so real, you could almost touch and smell them. Back in the kitchen, she turned on the radio to hear the latest news and the weather forecast. Then she began cleaning and dicing the fruit she picked up at Brynn's Pantry earlier in the day.

Her nose wrinkled as a pungent smell drifted under the laundry room door into the kitchen—cigar smoke! She shook her head. Just because Joe's family had received money from the church (Seymour's money) didn't mean Joe could go around wasting it on booze and smelly cigars. It wasn't that long ago Betty was shopping at the food bank just to feed the family. Joe should be thinking ahead now that the meat-packing plant was closing.

Thinking about Joe Chadwick, she almost jumped out of her shoes when the laundry room door opened and Joe stepped into the kitchen. She gasped, holding her hand over her heart.

"Sorry to startle you," he said, taking off his Blue Jay's cap and pushing his sweaty hair back under it. "I'll be off now, but I'll be back in the morning to put Polyfilla in the holes."

"Thanks, Joe. I guess my mind is elsewhere. We've got a full house this weekend. Guests will be arriving tomorrow afternoon, and the new washer and dryer will be delivered at 11:00."

"No worries," Joe said. I'll be here early and out of your hair by 10:00." He headed back out through the laundry room door.

She looked out the kitchen window, the sill lined with various potted herbs, and watched as he got into his truck and drove away. It was raining now. The weatherman had called for heavy rain for the long weekend. She was hoping his upcoming forecast—didn't hold water.

Still looking outside, a large crow caught her attention as it landed in the maple tree just outside the window. Soon it was joined by another, then another. And as the third landed in the tree, she tried to remember the myth about crows Brynn had told her (another one of Brynn's grandma Mumsie's superstitions). She counted them as they landed. One crow was unlucky, two good luck, three meant a family member would die. Oh no! Thank goodness a fourth landed. What was that, oh yes, four meant financial gain. Good, she thought, hoping it stopped there. Then, a fifth landed—sickness. And finally, a sixth came in for a landing. She counted just to make sure—one, two, three, four, five... six! Her brows merged together, and her face twisted. Six meant death! Goosebumps ran up and down her arms. Shaking the jitters out, she told herself it was only a stupid superstition. Then she bent down, grabbed two pots from under the sink, slid the window open and whacked the pots together. The birds took off. Rolling her eyes, she closed the window and got back to the business at hand.

With her pies finally ready to go into the oven, she put them on a large cookie sheet, reached down, and opened the oven door. An ear-deafening boom and a shockwave of hell-scorching heat knocked her off her feet. Sending her body flying through the air amidst wood, glass, and steel, all dancing around her in a fiery waltz.

CHAPTER THIRTY-SIX

Prissy

(Saturday, June 30)

JUST OFF THE MAIN highway, carved into a large limestone slab hidden behind a giant oak tree was the entrance to Rosehaven Academy. When Prissy had first spotted it from the windows of the van bringing her to this so-called school, she worried the sign would be easily missed if anyone came looking for her. The van continued on down a long, winding, road through dense woods on either side, and stopped in front of a large, stately yellow-brick manor, surrounded by manicured lawns and colourful flowerbeds.

Prissy sat on the bed, listening to the rain outside, pillows propped up behind her, and looked around the room. She'd now been at the facility for almost a week. Her room, was small, with just a twin bed, desk, chair, and tiny closet. At least, she didn't have to share it with anyone like bitchy Charlotte, who claimed to have parents with megabucks. They'd sent her to the school just so they could travel around the world and not have to worry about her. Or like Shamika who was always crying her head off because she missed her stupid boyfriend. Since Prissy was the same age as these two girls, the counsellors tried getting them together, hoping they'd become friends. Fat chance that was going to happen.

She still couldn't believe her parents had stuck her in this place. Yes, it looked nice— walking trails, a pool, a gym and more—but that didn't fool her. With a gazillion rules, this was way worse than regular school. Yet she'd done nothing wrong. She wasn't the problem for shit's sake—her parents were!

Her egocentric mom cared about only three things—herself (top of the list), money and their family's status in the community. Prissy knew she could never live up to her mother's image of the perfect daughter. She sure as hell didn't even come close. And her dad was hardly ever around, and when he was, he was either following the stock market, had his nose buried in the newspaper, or he was on his phone. Who could blame him? Her mom was a dragon lady.

The first days here were a nightmare. She'd refused help from the so-called caring teachers and counsellors and wouldn't participate in the daily routines. They were lame. There were set times for: classes, study periods, homework, exercise, counseling, meals, and bedtime. If the staff could, they'd even schedule pee breaks!

She'd made life hell for everyone, hoping they would kick her out. She'd been mouthy and rude, which had been kind of fun, and once had even thrown food at a teacher. That was hysterical. It felt like Big Brother was watching her 24/7. The counselling sessions had been the worst:

"Why do you think you're here, Prissy?" the shrink had asked as he gawked at her like she was a bug under a microscope that he couldn't identify.

With a shrug, she'd said squat, staring at her feet. She knew to make eye contact was a form of interaction. So she sat in the chair defiant, her arms folded across her chest. She refused to participate in this crazy charade.

"Prissy? You'll feel better once we can get to the root of the problem."

Chuckling to herself, she'd remembered a joke a friend told her and repeated the joke to the shrink:

"Hey, doc... you gotta help me!"

"What's the matter?"

"I keep having these recurring nightmares! It starts out where I'm sitting in a chair on my back porch, just rocking back and forth peacefully, enjoying the sunshine.

Suddenly, I realize I haven't had breakfast yet, and I get really excited about it.

So, I start to get up, but suddenly a screw pops out of my chair and the whole thing falls apart, sending me crashing to the ground. Then I wake up sweating!"

"I see... the doc says. Well, I think it's pretty obvious what the problem is."

"What? Tell me!"

"Clearly, you've got a screw loose, you're off your rocker, and you're cuckoo for Cocoa Puffs."

She and her friend had laughed their heads off, but the psychiatrist sitting across from her, just sat there stone faced. No sense of humour at all. Then in a voice devoid of emotion, he said their session was over.

Sundays were visitors day. She figured her parents knew the wound was too fresh, and that she's just rip them apart, so they didn't come. But she did take her dad's phone call afterward just to tell him off. Would they be here tomorrow?

Finally, she realized the only person she was hurting with this behavior was herself—maybe if she conformed, they'd let her out of here. Even though she'd never admit it, she did like the school's Drama and Repertoire Theatre Program, it was highly regarded, in the area. The kids put on performances in towns around the school. Real actors even showed up to teach a class from time to time.

She'd balked at joining the drama class at first, but then she'd figured it was preferable to taking some other stupid classes like Economics or, God forbid, Religious Studies. Just for the heck of it, she'd tried out for the part of Audrey in "Little Shop of Horrors," and she'd beat out six other girls for the part. The boy who played Seymour (*her dad's name… geesh!*) was gorgeous and funny and, well, pretty cool. A far cry from sulky Dylan. They'd hit it off right away. His name was Jared Spencer.

Passing by the main office one afternoon, she'd noticed it was empty, and she nonchalantly wandered in. The key to the filing cabinet was sticking out of the top drawer. She rifled through the drawers and found Jared's file. He was twenty, had an IQ of 140 (a near freakin' genius), and was "doing time" for cyber addiction and alcohol abuse. She shoved the file back in the drawer when she heard voices coming down the hall, then quickly slipped out of the office undetected.

That night, she was still smiling when she flopped into bed. For the first time since the hulks had brought her to this hellhole, she hadn't thought about Dylan at all.

CHAPTER THIRTY-SEVEN

Brynn

(Saturday, June 30)

SLOWLY, I BACKED INTO the store, shaking off my sopping-wet umbrella and shutting the door behind me. I flipped the sign on the door over to "Open," even though I wasn't really expecting many customers today. After leaving my umbrella on the porch, I headed to the back of the shop to hang my raincoat up in the bathroom.

The farmers in the area had been praying for rain for the last couple of months, and they finally got it—in biblical proportions. This was the third day of torrential rain. The county was basically an island attached to the mainland by two bridges, one at either end, and the winter run-off had flooded many of the homes along the water's edge. The water level had finally started receding, but now with this deluge, people were starting to worry again.

I took my raincoat off, admiring it and thinking what a wonderful gift Sophie had given me on my last birthday. This beautiful black Joules raincoat was covered with little cats and dogs all holding tiny yellow umbrellas, and to top it off, it had come with a little matching raincoat for Chewie.

My birthday being in April, it always seemed to rain. When I was very little, one birthday, I was quite upset because I wanted to play outside, but couldn't because ... surprise, it was raining. Then, my mother told me a story. She said it was the sky crying because it had lost one of its most beautiful and precious angels, who went to earth to become someone's little girl. I never minded the rain after that.

Still wearing my rubber boots, I went into the hydroponic room to see if Joe Chadwick fixed the defective overhead grow light. It's constant flickering was driving me crazy. Joe had been an electrician in the army and still did a few odd jobs when he was sober. Sam hired him to do the lighting and wiring for our hydroponic garden.

I opened the large, insulated door into the room, and, as always, was amazed at the lush greenery: tomatoes, lettuce, spinach, green peppers, basil, thyme and even a variety of flowers. It seemed miraculous that they could grow without soil, just water and nutrients. Kind of like the plasma bags you get hooked up to in the hospital. I was disappointed when I hit the switch and the one grow light was still flickering.

I texted him. A few seconds later it chirped a reply:

"Probably just a loose bulb that needs tightening."

Not wanting him to come all the way over on such a lousy day just to tighten a bulb, I texted him back:

"Okay, I'll tighten it. Thanks."

I grabbed the ladder I saw leaning against the far wall and set it up under the flickering light. I knew that LED bulbs weren't hot to the touch, so, after climbing up, I reached up and gave it a twist.

I felt a searing, painful vibration travel throughout my whole body. It felt like being stung by a two-hundred-pound bee... then everything went black.

The door-bell tinkled as Lori-Anne entered the shop. She knew Brynn was here because she saw her umbrella out on the porch, the front door was unlocked and the sign on the door was flipped to "Open." She was surprised at how quiet and empty the place was. The light behind the counter hadn't been turned on yet, and the sound of the coffeemaker usually chugging away was missing. No radio could be heard spouting the morning news. Probably running late because of all the rain, she thought. She put her umbrella on the porch next to Brynn's, then headed to the back, sticking her head into the darkened kitchen as she passed by, calling out, "Brynn! Where are you?"

No reply.

In the washroom, she saw Brynn's rain coat hanging on a hook and figured she was probably in the hydroponic room across the hall. Pushing the heavy door open, she scanned the room calling Brynn's name. She was surprised the grow lights were all off here as well, and tried flicking the switch. Nothing happened. Then, looking down one of the aisles, she noticed the aluminum ladder lying on the floor and went to check it out. She froze for a split-second, her mouth falling open when she saw Brynn lying on the concrete floor, her head surrounded by a pool of blood. She quickly knelt down beside her, pulled out her cell and dialed 911.

CHAPTER THIRTY-EIGHT

Brynn

(Sunday, July 1)

I AWOKE IN AN unfamiliar bed. The first thing I saw when my eyes fluttered open and finally focused was Sam's face, hovering above me, etched with worry.

"Hi, there," he said, his mouth curving into a smile. "Welcome back."

I tried to speak, but nothing came out.

He quickly raised the head of my bed, then filled the plastic cup on the bedside table from the water jug sitting there and held it up to my lips.

I took a sip and managed to rasp out, "Thank you," as I looked around the room. "Am I in hospital?"

"Yes, you're lucky to be alive. You had a nasty electrical shock at the store. The only thing that saved you were those rubber boots you were wearing."

"I remember being on the ladder, then—"

"Well, thank God for those rubber boots." He leaned over and kissed my forehead. I winced, feeling pain shoot through my right hand as I tried pushing myself up. Then noticed my hand was all wrapped up in gauze bandages.

"Careful now," Sam said, reaching behind me and adjusting my pillows. "You've got a bad burn on your hand, and one on your foot. Your body became part of the electrical current when it came into contact. The current entered your body through your hand and exited through your foot. And you have a pretty bad gash on your forehead from falling off the ladder. You hit your head on the concrete floor—it took about thirty stitches to close it up.

I looked at him, bewildered.

He smiled at me and gave me another sip of water.

You also have a mild concussion. The doctors have done a number of tests for any possible damage the shock may have done to your heart or other organs. Thankfully, all the tests came back negative. They still want to do a couple more, but, honey, I'd say you're one lucky girl!"

Looking at Sam shifting around uneasily in his seat, I knew he had something else to tell me. "What? What haven't you told me?" I asked.

His sad eyes looked at me. "I'm sorry, sweetheart, but there's more bad news—I know you wouldn't want me to hold anything back." He cleared his throat and leaned in closer. "Georgie had a terrible accident. It looks like the gas stove in her kitchen exploded when she went to use it. She survived, but she's in hospital as well—in a coma and just hanging on. Her outcome isn't looking good."

My heart raced. "No, this can't be happening *again*—is she here—in this hospital? I need to see her!"

Sam nodded, saw me trying to get out of bed, and put his arm out, stopping me. "You're not in any shape. You can barely move."

"Yes, I can," I said, pushing his arm away. I climbed out of bed, feeling a little unsteady on my feet. Sam reached for me, but I waved him away. "Just go get me a wheelchair." He knew better than to argue with me and left the room to find one. He was back within minutes and helped me into it.

"She's in Room 39, just down the hall," he said.

He wheeled me along the corridor. As we entered the room, we saw Georgie's husband, Hugh, sitting by her bedside, slumped in a chair, eyes closed, elbows resting on his knees.

When he heard us come in, he looked up, then came over, his eyes wet and puffy, and gave us each a hug. "How are you doing, Brynn?"

"Don't worry about me, I'm as tough as old boots. How's she doing?" I asked, wheeling myself over to Georgie's bedside.

"Not so well, it's touch-and-go. She's in a coma, which in this case is a mercy. Her face is mangled, she's lost sight in one eye, and she has burns to over sixty percent of her body." He pulled a handkerchief out of his pants pocket and blew his nose.

Sam put his arm around Hugh's shoulders.

I just sat there, grief-stricken, my physical pain forgotten.

˜

The next morning I was back at home sitting in the living room wrapped in a blanket recuperating. TV on for background noise. The front doorbell chimed. As I got up and hobbled my way over to the door, Chewie jumped down from the couch and did his usual circus bit—dancing and barking—hindering my progress.

"Chewie quiet," I shouted… "sit'!" He sat, making a whiny noise, his large eyes darting between me and the front door. As I opened the door, he dashed out and resumed barking at the intruder. Chief Boyd bent down and gave him a good petting.

"Sorry, Charlie," I said, "we're still in the puppy training stage. Obviously, we haven't gotten far."

Charlie straightened up and did a double-take when he saw my bandaged head, hand, and foot. "Boy, I'd hate to see the other guy," he said, taking off his hat and smiling. I waved him in. Chewie was right on his heels. "I just stopped by to see how you're doing and fill you in on the latest news."

Offering him a drink, which he declined, we went into the living-room. He took a seat beside the couch which was littered with my blankets and pillow. I pushed them aside and lowered myself down.

"So how are you, really?" he asked.

"I'm doing fine. Everyone says how lucky I am. I guess that was a really stupid thing I did. I'm on pain meds now, so I can hardly feel the burns on my hand and foot. At the moment I only have a little bit of tingling and itchiness. On the whole—pretty good."

"I'm glad to hear it," he said. "I guess there's still no change in Georgie's condition?"

"Unfortunately, no, but she's still hanging in there. We're all praying for her."

The warm smile on his face disappeared, replaced by a serious look. "I hate to be the bearer of *more* bad news," he said, closing his eyes.

My stomach dropped as I stared at him.

He opened his eyes, a pained look on his face. "We've found Trish. I'm sorry to tell you this Brynn, but Trish is dead. We checked the DNA on the body parts we found, and they were a match."

"Body parts—oh, my God! My legs went weak. "What happened? Was she in an accident?"

I could tell he was hesitant to continue, seeing the look of horror on my face.

"It's okay, go on," I said, not really wanting him to, but needing to know.

"It looks like a homicide. A couple of workers at the mushroom farm were picking what they thought were mushrooms, but to their horror, discovered that the so-called mushrooms turned out to be body parts! They found toes, fingers, a nose. It looks like her body went through the thrasher, and parts were dispersed out through the large electric fan spreader into the growing compound. I'm so sorry."

With my hands covering my gaping mouth, I sat there in disbelief.

Charlie continued. "This sheds a whole new light on things. We know for certain you women are being targeted.

My head couldn't stop shaking like I had some kind of palsy. "But, my accident was because of my own stupidity."

Chief Boyd looked at me. "I don't think so. The investigators noticed a hole drilled right above the light fixture where the rainwater dripped in on a cracked part of the housing. That caused the short. Looks like it was intentional.

"I can't believe this!"

"I shouldn't be telling you, but seeing as you were the one who brought the evidence items in. The smashed piece of plastic you found in the Oldenbergs' backyard was a voice changer. Could have been bought anywhere, even on-line through Amazon. It can even change a man's voice to sound like a woman's, and vice versa. We're doing a finger print analysis on it, and, the Forensic Department is working on trying to decipher the real voice on the phone. The crumpled-up cigarette pack was an empty pack of Winchester cigarillos, and the piece of metal you found in the locker room at the mushroom farm was a shim, probably used to open the combination lock."

"We're holding Joe Chadwick in custody at the moment on a drunk and disorderly charge. But we have our suspicions about him. What we need and don't have is hard evidence. If nothing comes up, he'll be out by tomorrow.

"Joe! Why would Joe want to harm us? It doesn't make sense?"

Putting his hat on, he stood up to leave. He gave Chewy a pat on the head on his way to the front door. "Joe can't account for his whereabouts on the nights in question, and we know he has psychological issues. I wanted you to be aware of the danger you're in. So, be careful, and in the meantime, if you see a squad car tailing you, it's for your own safety. We'll also be keeping a watchful eye on Sophie and Georgie."

After he left, I scrunched down in the sofa, feeling the hair on the back of my neck standing on end. Chewy jumped up and snuggled next to me. My mind was working overtime trying to come up with who would possibly want us dead that much! Sure, we took Seymour's money and still ratted on him, but what's the point of getting rid of us now? And Lara, she's all bark and no bite. Joe Chadwick? The more I thought about him, the more I realized he'd had a connection to most of the incidents that happened. He knew the Hendriks' farm well enough and even helped out there occasionally. He also knew the Oldenbergs' place, and Mrs. Pierce said he'd trapped strays for them before. He supposedly fixed the faulty light fixture at my store and, he was at the Fenwoods' doing work in the laundry room the afternoon of the explosion. I tilted my head mentally weighing the evidence. "Oh my God . . . could it be? I looked down at Chewy, his little, warm body squashed beside me as I sat there, my eyes wet with tears.

I remembered Betty telling me that shortly after they were married, Joe was diagnosed—unofficially mind you—as bipolar. If he'd been officially diagnosed in the army, they would have discharged him, so they kept it a secret. When he got home from Kandahar, after witnessing the horrors of war and losing two of his buddies and his foot, he was diagnosed with PTSD. I realized he was a bit of a loose cannon, especially when he was drinking—who knows what's going on in his head? But why want us dead, if anything, we're the ones that have been helping his family. I lowered my head, hands covering my face.

Suddenly, bolting upright, it dawned on me: Sophie was part of the clean-up crew at the meat-packing plant today. With my pulse racing, I stood up—I just had to get over there. Hobbling over to the hall mirror, I was shocked at the person staring back at me. I took a tissue from my pocket and dabbed at my wet eyes; grabbed my hairbrush from my purse and ran it through my hair. Chewy came running into the hall just as I was putting my coat on. "No, Chewie, sorry, you can't come with me today, buddy." I reached into the fancy ceramic jar sitting on the hall table, grabbed a couple of doggie biscuits, threw them on the floor and limped out the door.

CHAPTER THIRTY-NINE

Sophie

(Sunday, July 1)

THE LOUD BEEP, BEEP, beeping sound of the alarm clock woke Sophie up. She reached out from under the covers to turn it off but accidentally knocked it off the nightstand. The clock hit the hardwood floor with a clunk and, like the Energizer Bunny, just kept beeping.

"Alright, you made your point already," she muttered. Throwing the covers back, she got up, reached down and grabbed the annoying thing. After giving it the evil eye, she smacked it back down on the nightstand. Not used to getting up early on a Sunday, she reluctantly made her way into the bathroom to get ready for work.

Although she normally worked Monday and Thursday afternoons, today she was asked to go in and help with the final cleanup before the plant closed for good. She hadn't minded working at the meat plant; the extra money came in handy now that her husband Stanley's workman's comp had run out. She felt bad about the meat plant closing, especially for her coworkers who had young families to support.

She heard Stanley puttering about downstairs and smelled the coffee brewing. It reminded her of an article she read recently about how just smelling coffee powers up the brain. Apparently, a study was done with rats, comparing the rodents who sniffed coffee with those that didn't. Those who sniffed the coffee had more energy. Maybe, she thought, chuckling to herself, one only had to stick one's nose in a jar of coffee, take a whiff— say around 3:00 in the afternoon, when your energy started to lag—and you'd perk right up.

After getting washed and dressed, she headed downstairs. Stan was in the kitchen at the stove, frying eggs. She didn't know how long he'd been up but figured he had another restless night. His back pain kept him awake.

"Morning, doll," he said, looking over at her smiling. She knew he was in pain most of the time, but he never complained.

"Morning, dearie," she said, going over and giving him a peck on the cheek. She then reached into the cupboard and pulled down her coffee mug with a picture of the late great Snowball on it. She remembered when Sam saw her coffee mug; he had one made for Brynn with Chewie's picture on it—they both loved their mutt mugs.

After a quick breakfast, she grabbed her gear and, not wanting to be late for work (it being the last day), kissed Stanley again and flew out the door.

∽

With only a skeleton crew working on the cleanup, the plant was quiet. The lighting in the plant was dim, except down back, where the large machinery was located—it was all lit up like a hospital operating theatre.

She headed straight to the maintenance closet, pulled on her coveralls, put the cleaning supplies she needed in a bucket, and made her way down towards the machines. Her co-worker, Dougie, was already hard at work. The pungent odor of chlorine bleach filled the air.

"Morning, Sophie," he said. "So, you're in on this cleanup too, eh?"

"Yes, I'm not sure where to start."

"You best go see Tony over there." He pointed toward the main line equipment at the back of the plant.

As she made her way down to see Tony, the floor supervisor, she could see up into Seymour's office through the large picture window overlooking the plant floor below. Seymour, appeared to be in a heated argument with Joe Chadwick. Sophie wondered what on earth they were arguing about when Tony came up beside her.

"Oh, mornin' Tony," she said. "Where would you like me ta start cleaning?"

"You can start with the Hamster. Mr. Harding said a woman would be best cleaning it because of their smaller hands—better to get into the tight areas inside the machine. Follow me, and I'll show you what needs doing."

Sophie remembered the day they got the machine. It was the latest in robotic technology. Seymour had almost popped his buttons, strutting around with his chest puffed out with pride. Few packing plants could afford the expensive HAMGAS-R, which they nicknamed "the Hamster." They touted it as being able to debone five hundred hams an hour, where skilled butchers could only debone around fifty. She thought… progress, yes, but at what cost—lost jobs, that's what!

At the end of each of the robotic arms were razor-sharp knives, with springs on either side of the blades that mimicked a human's wrist movements. The springs allowed the blades to follow the contours of the bone and grain in the meat closely, reducing waste. X-rays analyzed each pork thigh on the production line. With X-rays, the robot could detect the shape of the joint, and imitate the work of human hands. A control system used eight markers and got as close to the bone as possible. The robot could even determine a right leg from a left.

Jokes flew around the plant after the Hamster arrived, when an article in the *Technovision Magazine* told about another robot being developed that could detect what things smelled like. It was subsequently tested by the article writer. He put his hand under the machine and it came out smelling like pork. The employees imaginations ran wild with this one. What if AI developed to the point where the Hamster and this E-nose machine were merged and became mobile . . . *geesh*!

The floor supervisor showed Sophie the diagram of the machine and the various parts that needed cleaning. Some of the parts could be disassembled and dropped into a bucket of cleaning solvent, and a special pressure washer cleaned most of the rest. However, some parts inside the main body of the machine needed to be done by hand.

"Don't worry Sophie, the power is off," Tony joked.

She rolled her eyes. "Well, that's good ta know, boy-o."

As she headed back to the maintenance room to get more supplies, she happened to glance out the window overlooking the parking lot and saw Brynn and Lara in a heated exchange. She wondered what the heck was going on. Shrugging, she turned back to the job at hand, telling herself she'd ask Brynn about it later.

Sophie had finished cleaning the Hamster's exterior and was just about to start work on the interior when from the corner of her eye she saw Lara Harding down on the floor. That was unusual! Lara had come to the plant many times, but she'd never seen her down here on the plant floor before. She shrugged, then got back to the job at hand. She leaned over the conveyor belt and began reaching into the machine—

It suddenly jumped to life!

She jerked her hand back, her heart in her throat. The next thing she knew, someone was grabbing her from behind and trying to shove her onto the conveyor belt.

Sophie fought back, but being a slight ninety-seven pounds, it was a losing battle. Then, just as abruptly, she was let go and tumbled to the floor. When she rolled over and looked back up, she couldn't believe her eyes. Lara was wrestling with Brynn, and it looked like Lara was now trying to shove Brynn up onto the fast-moving belt.

Joe Chadwick suddenly appeared out of nowhere. He wrangled Brynn out of Lara's clutches, and somehow in the scuffle, Lara ended up on her back on the conveyor belt, moving quickly towards the machine opening. Her long black hair, usually done up in a tidy bun, had come loose during her struggles and was now splayed out on the conveyor belt. It got tangled up in the metal grippers at the mouth of the machine. Joe tried to pull her off the belt, but with all her kicking and screaming—he couldn't get near her.

Joe sprinted toward the control room and the emergency power off (EPO) kill switch. But, before he could get there, a blood-curdling scream reverberated throughout the plant. Lara was now being pulled into the machine, head first. The rest of her body, arms, and legs thrashed about outside on the belt. Inside the X-rays measured her head from top to bottom, side to side, determining the precise individual sections to cut. The first cut went through her neck, bone and all, leaving her headless body bouncing around outside on the conveyor belt. Then, the cutting arms inside the machine, each made a fresh cut as the head moved along the line. At the end of the line, the machine flung out a perfectly cut head of ham!

CHAPTER FORTY

Brynn

(Two weeks later)

GEORGIE WAS NOW HOME, beginning her long road to recovery. Sophie and I sat by her bedside. It was now two weeks since the dreadful events at the meat packing plant.

My eyes teared up, looking at Georgie lying there, wrapped in bandages from head to toe, one eye closed, the other covered by a patch. An intravenous line dangled from a pole and disappeared between the bandages on her arm.

"She's a strong lass; she'll be okay." Sophie said, grabbing my hand and squeezing it. "I still don't know how you figured out Lara was the killer!"

"Unfortunately, I wish I had known sooner. At one point, it really looked like Joe Chadwick had succumbed to his PTSD and gone completely off the deep end. But after Chief Boyd told me that he had confessed to the hit-and-run, I realized he was already a broken man, how would he benefit from doing away with us women? And Seymour's alibi for the hit and run held water. He really was golfing that weekend.

But he thought his wife had driven his car; that's why he tried to buy our silence. And Lara was covering up for her daughter, who she thought was the hit-and-run driver." I took a sip from my water bottle. "Talk about a Shakespearean tragedy! Dylan finally admitted that Prissy drove her dad's car over to his house the night of the accident. Who knows, maybe Prissy actually thought she *had* hit the kid? That girl's trouble at the best of times. But I never thought she was involved in the murders, and besides, she was at the boarding school the night of the stove explosion. Now, her mother—"

Sophie stared at me as she leaned in closer. "I saw Joe up in the office on cleanup day arguing with Seymour. He was really upset, face red, arms flying around; then he stormed out of the room."

Shaking my head in disbelief, I looked down at Georgie lying there. "Obviously, Lara had mental issues we weren't aware of. She would do anything to protect her daughter and their family's reputation. And with her geology degree and having worked in her father's fracking business, she would have knowledge of and access to explosives. Chief Boyd said plastic explosives with a motion detector were used at the Fenwicks'—so when the oven door was opened! Other things fell into place too—Lara was eavesdropping when Edda was telling me about her husband and sons being out of town at a conference. Lara also saw firsthand how frightened and allergic Kaydee was of cats. She probably found out from Prissy, who was friends with Kym, that the Oldenbergs had lots of cats and would be out of town for a few days."

"But what I don't understand," Sophie said, is why Kaydee's inhaler was empty and she didn't have her EpiPen with her?"

"Well, you know what it's like in the county—no one locks their doors. I'm sure Lara took advantage of that. She had the opportunity when she was collecting for the book drive. And Hugh said she was hanging around in their kitchen, having a drink of water, while he went searching for the books for the book drive.

"I'm certainly locking my door after this!" Sophie said, folding her arms across her chest in defiance. Then, softening her tone, she asked. "And what about Trish? How would Lara know Trish and Dylan would be working in the same room that night?"

"Well, remember Georgie telling us she bumped into Lara at the mushroom farm? Lara probably looked at the work schedule on the wall while she was there and must have called Dylan, pretending to be from the office, telling him not to bother coming in."

"But how would Lara have the strength to move Trish's body outside? And how…" Sophie asked, scratching her chin, "would she have managed getting the body into the thrashing machine?"

"I'm just guessing here," I said, shrugging, but it's possible she put the body in the trolley cart and pushed it outside. Lara's pretty fit. Then, there's a conveyor belt that takes the hay and fertilizer mixture up to the thrasher."

Georgie stirred, moaning a little, and opened her eye.

We both stopped talking and looked over at her.

"Hey, Georgie," I said. "Did you have a good sleep?"

Georgie wet her lips… "Sleep? Not Sleeping Beauty," she mumbled.

Sophie quickly got up and poured a glass of water, put a straw in it, and took it over to her. After taking a sip, Georgie gave us a weak smile, closed her eye and nodded off again.

EPILOGUE

Brynn

(September)

IT WAS THE END of September now, and things were getting back to normal in Hubbs Harbour. The front door bell tinkled an arrival as Sophie shouldered her way in carrying a large cardboard box filled with pint boxes of fresh blueberries.

"Here, let me give you a hand with that," I said. "You shouldn't be carrying that big box. If I'd known, I would have come and gotten it from your car."

"I'm no lag," she said, frowning. She carried the box across the room and plopped it on the counter. "Have you heard anything more about how the Chadwicks are doing?"

"Considering Joe Chadwick caused the death of his own son, while driving under the influence—he got off relatively lightly. He pleaded guilty. The judge must have taken pity on him, Joe being a war vet and already suffering from accidentally killing his son. He gave him just three years' probation with community service. He's been ordered to attend AA and take a mandatory drivers education course. He's also being treated for his PTSD.

"How's the wee lassie?" Sophie enquired.

"Things are better for Deedee, too. The treatments on her face are working well; you can see the difference already. The angry-looking blueish blotch is fading and is a lot smoother. And some good news," I continued. "Joe has started a new job. Dave McCauley hired him to sell used cars at the Ford dealership. Turns out Joe's a good salesman. He's back home now, and things are looking up for the family. He hasn't had a drink for three months."

"Wonderful! It's about time that family got a break. Any more news from Dylan out in L.A.?"

"You're not going to believe this, but Betty heard from him a few days ago—he's got an acting job in a new upcoming TV pilot. It's scheduled to hit the air waves in the spring. He met an actress out there while they were both working at a donut shop. She persuaded him to go with her to an open audition for the show. She didn't get a part, but he got the lead!"

Sophie gave a whistle. "Wow, that's something all right. I hate to ask, but do you know what's happening with the Hardings?"

"Seymour and his receptionist Bunny have moved in together. Prissy met a guy at the boarding school and is now living with him on his family's farm over in Brunswick. I heard they are planning to get married."

"It's hard to believe that our dear friends Edda, Kaydee, and Trish are gone." I said, a wave of sadness washing over me. "If only we had known our decision to remain silent would go so horrendously wrong.

"Aye, a real tragedy! I'm glad the church is holding a special memorial service for our dear lost sisters at the arena this Saturday. I'm sure all of Hubb's Harbour will turn out."

"How was your latest visit with Georgie?" I asked. "How is she doing?"

"She's better. Poor lass will be needing a lot of reconstructive surgery, and the doctors hope the eye patch she's wearing can eventually be replaced with a glass eye. She's a fighter, that one!"

"You know, Soph, when bad things happen, you've still got to go on. Try to have something good grow from the ashes of what you loved so much. Life goes on. Our church has been saved, soon you won't even know that little Deedee had a disfigurement, and the Chadwicks are doing well now that Joe is back home and off the booze. *And,* I'm pregnant—fingers crossed! Maybe there's a thread of gold in our misled silence." A tear trickled down my cheek. "It's sad to say, but sometimes bad things happen to good people.

The End

ACKNOWLEDGEMENTS

I want to express my gratitude to my beta readers: Roxanne MacKenzie, Beverly Skidmore, Rick McPhail, Virginia Hair, and my husband, Gunter—my toughest critic. Also, a big thanks to my editor, Joy Goddard, and the editors at Amazon.

A shout out to my writing group sponsored by the Prince Edward County Public Library and led by Andrew Binks. Your encouragement has meant a lot—thanks guys!

ABOUT THE AUTHOR

Sharon Stefan has worked as a secretary and administrator for many years while harbouring a dream of becoming a novelist. In her spare time, she scribbled down words and chapters in a notebook, finally culminating in Silence is ~~Golden~~ Deadly her first novel.

Sharon lives with her husband in Prince Edward County, Ontario and continues to write and enjoys exploring all the County has to offer.